Robert B. Parker

"PARKER IN TOP-NOTCH FORM."
—*The Seattle Times*

A Spenser Novel

Hundred-Dollar Baby

BERKLEY

$9.99 U.S.
$13.50 CAN

ISBN 978-0-425-21755-9

S ▷ EAN

continued . . .

Hundred-Dollar Baby

·$·

ROBERT B. PARKER

BERKLEY BOOKS
New York

THE BERKLEY PUBLISHING GROUP
Published by the Penguin Group
Penguin Group (USA) Inc.
375 Hudson Street, New York, New York 10014, USA
Penguin Group (Canada), 90 Eglinton Avenue East, Suite 700, Toronto, Ontario M4P 2Y3, Canada
(a division of Pearson Penguin Canada Inc.)
Penguin Books Ltd., 80 Strand, London WC2R 0RL, England
Penguin Group Ireland, 25 St. Stephen's Green, Dublin 2, Ireland (a division of Penguin Books Ltd.)
Penguin Group (Australia), 250 Camberwell Road, Camberwell, Victoria 3124, Australia
(a division of Pearson Australia Group Pty. Ltd.)
Penguin Books India Pvt. Ltd., 11 Community Centre, Panchsheel Park, New Delhi—110 017, India
Penguin Group (NZ), 67 Apollo Drive, Rosedale, North Shore 0745, Auckland, New Zealand
(a division of Pearson New Zealand Ltd.)
Penguin Books (South Africa) (Pty.) Ltd., 24 Sturdee Avenue, Rosebank, Johannesburg 2196,
South Africa

Penguin Books Ltd., Registered Offices: 80 Strand, London WC2R 0RL, England

This is a work of fiction. Names, characters, places, and incidents either are the product of the author's imagination or are used fictitiously, and any resemblance to actual persons, living or dead, business establishments, events, or locales is entirely coincidental. The publisher does not have any control over and does not assume any responsibility for author or third-party websites or their content.

HUNDRED-DOLLAR BABY

A Berkley Book / published by arrangement with the author

PRINTING HISTORY
G. P. Putnam's Sons hardcover edition / October 2006
Berkley premium edition / September 2007

ISBN: 978-0-425-21755-9

PRINTED IN THE UNITED STATES OF AMERICA

10 9 8 7 6 5 4 3 2 1

For Joan: Priceless

· 1 ·

The woman who came into my office on a bright January day was a knockout. Her hair had blond highlights and her fawn-colored suit appeared to have been hand-sewn by Michael Kors. She took off some sort of fur-lined cape and tossed it over the arm of my couch, and came over and sat down in one of my client chairs. She smiled at me. I smiled at her. She waited. The light coming in my window was especially bright this morning, enhanced by the light snowfall that had collected overnight. She didn't seem dangerous. I remained calm.

"You don't know who I am," she said after a while. "Do you."

Her voice sounded as if it had been polished by old money. It was her eyes. Someone I knew was in there behind those eyes.

"Not yet," I said.

She smiled.

" 'Not yet,' " she said. "That's so you. 'I don't know now, but I will.' "

"My glass is always half full," I said. "Are you going to tell me or do I have to frisk you."

"God, it's good to see you," she said. "It's April."

I stared at her. And then there she was.

"April Kyle," I said, and stood up.

She stood up, too. I walked around the desk and she almost jumped against me. I put my arms around her. She was beautiful, but the incest taboo had kicked in the moment I knew who she was. It was like hugging a little girl. All the cool elegance was gone. She stayed against me with her arms around me and pressed her face against my chest.

"It's like coming home," she said.

"When you have to go there, they have to take you in," I said.

"Robert Frost."

"Very good," I said.

"You taught me that," she said.

I nodded. She kept her face pressed against my chest. It made her voice muffle a little.

"You taught me almost everything I know that matters," she said.

"That's not so hard," I said. "Because not many things matter."

"But the ones that do," she said, "matter a lot."

She let me go and stood back and looked at me for a moment, then sat back down. I went back to my desk chair and tilted back in it.

"Are you still with Susan?" she said.

"Yes."

She nodded. "And you're still doing what you do."

"And charmingly," I said.

"You look the same," she said.

"Is that good or bad?" I said.

"It's absolutely marvelous," she said. "It's been so long. I was terrified you wouldn't be here. But here you are. Looking the same. Full of irony and strength."

"You've become quite beautiful," I said.

"Thank you."

"And graceful," I said.

She smiled.

"Is it real?" I said.

"Mostly," she said.

I was quiet. I could smell her perfume. It smelled expensive. She was expensive. Everything about her: clothes, manner, makeup, the way she crossed her legs. The way she spoke.

"I'm still a whore," she said.

"And a very successful one," I said.

"Actually, I don't do so much of the, ah, hands-on anymore," she said and smiled at me. "I'm management now."

"It's what makes America great," I said.

"You don't disapprove," she said.

"I'm the guy sent you to Mrs. Utley," I said.

"You had no choice," April said. "I was a complete mess. You had to find someone to take care of me."

"How about you," I said. "Do you disapprove?"

"Disapprove?" April said. "I've been in this business since I was fifteen."

"Doesn't mean you approve," I said.

"And you sending me to the best madam in New York doesn't mean you approve," April said.

"I had to think about it a little because of you," I said. "And if it's among consenting adults and no one is demeaned—seems okay to me."

"Have you ever had sex with a whore?" April said.

"Not lately," I said.

"So maybe you do disapprove."

"Or maybe I'm such a chick magnet," I said, "that I never had time."

April smiled and looked for a moment at the bright morning hovering over Berkeley Street.

"Do you disapprove of me?" she said.

"No," I said. "I don't."

"I guess that's probably what I really was asking."

"Probably," I said.

"I've been back in Boston for more than a year," April said.

I nodded.

"I never called you."

I nodded again.

"I guess I was afraid you wouldn't still be you, and, maybe, I guess, I was afraid you wouldn't like it that I was still in the whore business."

"I think the current correct phrase," I said, "is *sex worker.*"

April shook her head a little.

"You used to say that a thing is what it is and not something else."

"I did," I said.

We were quiet again. She wanted me to help her out of whatever trouble she was in, but she didn't want to admit she was in trouble. Half the people who came into my office were that way.

I waited.

"Two years ago," April said, "she gave me some money and sent me up here."

"Patricia Utley," I said.

"Yes. You know her operation in New York?"

"Yes."

"She wanted me to open a branch up here," April said.

"And?"

"And I did. I bought a mansion in the Back Bay and hired the girls, and paid off the proper people, and . . . the whole thing."

"Big job," I said.

"Big payoff," she said. "The business is very successful. I'm making a lot of money for her, and a lot of money for me."

"Good," I said.

"It's an all-woman enterprise," April said. "Mrs. Utley, me, the girls, even the more-or-less non-sex staff, bartenders, food preparation, everyone is female. The only men anywhere are the clients, and for them it's like a private club."

I nodded. She stopped talking and looked though the window again. I waited.

"And now some men are trying to take it away from us," she said.

Aha!

· 2 ·

Hawk parked his Jaguar in a resident-only space in front of April's mansion. The sun was bright but without warmth. The weather was very cold, and it had kept the light snow cover from melting, so that the mall along Commonwealth Ave. was still clean and white, and what snow there was underfoot was crisp and dry like sand.

We sat for a moment with the motor running and the heater on, and looked at the house. It was a beauty, a town house on a corner, four stories high with a big semicircular glass-roofed atrium on the cross-street side.

"April doesn't know who it is that's trying to shake her down," I said. "It was an anonymous phone call. But when she told him no, a couple guys showed up the next day and disrupted, ah, the orderly flow of enterprise."

"And they kept showing up?"

I nodded.

"It's an all-woman enterprise," I said. "And it's tricky. They are, after all, an illegal enterprise. It's hard to call the cops."

"Ain't there bribe money spread around?" Hawk said.

"Yes. But it's effective only when there's not a lot of attention drawn."

Hawk nodded, looking at the house.

"Girl's got nice taste," Hawk said.

"Like you would know," I said.

"Who more tasteful than me?" Hawk said.

"I told her we'd come around and discourage the interlopers," I said. "Maybe see who they represent."

Hawk nodded slowly, still looking at the house.

"Bouncer at a whorehouse," Hawk said. "The capstone of my career. We getting paid?"

"Yes."

"How much?"

"We haven't established that yet."

"Free samples?" Hawk said.

"You'll have to negotiate that with the samplees," I said.

Hawk shut off the engine and we got out. I had on a sheepskin jacket. Hawk was wearing a black fur coat. It was maybe eight degrees, but not much wind and it didn't feel too bad in the short walk to the front door.

There was a front desk in the high foyer. A good-looking young woman in a tailored suit was at the desk. A discreet sign on the desk said *Concierge*. She looked a little nervous when we came in. There were doors off the foyer in all directions, and an elegant staircase that curved up toward the second floor.

"My name is Spenser," I said. "For April Kyle."

The concierge looked relieved. She picked up the phone and spoke, and almost at once a door opened behind her and April appeared, looking just as elegant as she had in my office.

"Thank God you're here," she said. "They're coming."

We were in the office. It was spartan. There was a big modern work desk against the back wall. Desks where two women sat working at computers. A bank of file cabinets stood along one wall. There was a bank of television monitors high on the wall above the door.

"For future reference," April said to the office workers, "these are the good guys."

The two women looked at us silently. April didn't introduce us. She was all business, as if stepping into her work space had made her someone else. Hawk and I took off our coats and hung them on a hat rack near the door.

"The monitors are for security cameras," she said. "The one in the center is on the front door."

"Who's coming," I said.

"The man called," April said.

Her voice was flat and didn't sound emotional, except that she spoke very swiftly.

"He said they were tired of waiting. He said they were coming."

"To remonstrate with you?" I said.

"Yes," April said. "He told me this time it would be worse."

"Probably not," I said.

"I won't give in," April said. "I won't. He can't have this."

"What they do last time?" Hawk said.

"They pushed past Doris on the desk, and went through the house interrupting the girls and their guests, chasing the guests out."

"Very bad for business," Hawk said.

"Yes," April said. "Those guests are unlikely to return."

"You have a gun?" I said.

"Yes. But I don't want to use it. I don't want either of you to use one. That would be the end of it if someone got shot here."

"It would," I said.

"This is a good business," April said. "A good woman's business. I'm not going to give it up because some man wants part of it."

Hawk was watching the monitor.

"Hidey ho," he said.

April looked up.

"Yes," she said. "That's them."

"You ladies go somewhere," I said to the office workers.

They looked at April. April nodded. The two women got up and went out a door behind April's desk.

"How about you, my feminist beauty?" I said.

She smiled. She didn't seem frightened.

"I'll stay," April said.

"Don't blame you," Hawk said. "Be fun to watch."

· 3 ·

They were both wearing dark overcoats. On the monitor one of them looked fat. They brushed past the concierge desk and headed for April's office. The door opened and in they came. In person, one of them *was* fat. The other guy had the thick upper body of a weight lifter.

The weight lifter said, "Time for another talk, whore lady. . . ."

He stopped and looked at Hawk and me.

"Who the fuck are you?" he said.

"I often wonder," I said. "Don't you? Sometimes at night when you're alone?"

"You ain't customers," the weight lifter said.

The fact that Hawk's coat was off and he was wearing a .44 Magnum in a shoulder holster was probably a clue. They had thought it was going to be another walk in the park. Both of them had their overcoats buttoned up. If they were carrying, it would take them five minutes to get their guns out.

"We be whorehouse security," Hawk said.

He seemed pleasant. Both of the overcoats stared at us. They seemed a little uneasy. Despite the pleasant overtones, Hawk didn't look like a guy who'd surrender easily.

The weight lifter said, "Whoever the fuck you are, take a walk. We got business with the head whore."

"Her name is Miss Kyle," I said.

The fat guy began to unbutton his overcoat.

"Leave it buttoned," I said.

The fat guy frowned. "Fuck you," he said.

Hawk stepped away from where he'd been leaning on a file cabinet and knocked the fat guy down with a single punch. The punch exploded on him so fast that the fat guy never got his hands up. He got to his hands and knees and stayed there, shaking his head slowly. The weight lifter's hands moved slightly, as if he wanted to unbutton his coat, but he didn't.

"So who sent you here to talk with Miss Kyle?" I said.

"I ain't talking to you," the weight lifter said.

I almost felt bad for him. He had come here assuming he was going to frighten a few prostitutes and maybe slap around some guy from Newton, in town for an early-afternoon quickie. He hadn't planned on us. And as things developed, he was beginning to realize that he and his pal were overmatched.

"You are talking to me," I said. "It's just a matter of when."

The fat guy got painfully to his feet. He didn't look at Hawk. Hawk had his gun in his hand. He let it hang by his side.

"I got nothing to say," the weight lifter muttered.

He was trying to be a stand-up guy. I slapped him across the face with my open hand. Behind me I heard April gasp. The weight lifter stepped back. It hurt. It was humiliating. But mostly it startled him. People in his circle didn't do a lot of slapping. He put his hands up toward his face and glanced at his fat friend.

"Who sent you here to talk with Miss Kyle?" I said.

The weight lifter was backing toward the door. Hawk stepped across and blocked it.

"I'm getting outta here," the weight lifter said.

I feinted at his stomach with my right fist. He dropped his hands and I slapped him with my left hand. And then with my right. He hunched and ducked his head and covered his face. I slapped him on the top of the head. He put his hands up to cover. I slapped him in the face again.

"Stop it," he said. "Stop it, stop it."

His face was mottled.

"Who sent you to talk with Miss Kyle?" I said.

"Ollie," he said.

"You know Ollie?" I said to April.

"No."

"Who do you talk to?" I said.

April shrugged.

"He never gives a name," she said. "Maybe it's Ollie. I have no way to know."

"Tell me about Ollie," I said to the weight lifter.

"Ollie's got a crew," the weight lifter said. "Me and Tank work with him."

"What's Ollie's last name?"

"DeMars."

"Where is Ollie located?" I said.

"Andrews Square," the weight lifter said.

There was some sort of odd anticipation in his voice. I realized he couldn't wait for us to try our stuff on Ollie. Ollie would show us.

"He's got a clubhouse there," the weight lifter said. "Storefront, used to be a chiropractor's office. Right off the square."

"Why is Ollie asking you to annoy these folks?" I said.

"I don't know."

I smacked him across the face with my open hand. He ducked back.

"Don't," he said. "I honest to God don't know. Ollie just says keep on them until they come around."

"Which means?"

"They'll talk business."

"With Ollie?"

"I don't know."

"What business?"

"I don't know."

"You know, Tank?" I said to the fat guy.

He shook his head.

"You agree with everything he told us?" I said.

The fat guy nodded.

"Okay," I said. "Hands on the wall, legs apart. You know how it works."

They did as I said, and I patted them down. I took a gun from each of them, and a wallet. I put the guns on April's desk. I took the driver's licenses from the wallets and handed the wallets back to them.

"Tell Ollie we'll drop by," I said.

"How 'bout my gun?" the weight lifter said.

"You guys will have to risk it back to Andrews Square unarmed," I said. "Beat it."

They didn't like leaving the guns. The guns mattered to them. But there was nothing they could do about it. They turned toward the door. Hawk still blocked their way. They stopped. Hawk put the muzzle of his gun against the nose of the weight lifter.

"Don't come back here," Hawk said.

Nobody moved. Then Hawk stepped aside and the two men went out. We watched them through the front door and out onto the street.

"Thank you," April said when we were alone.

"It's not over," I said. "These two dopes may not return, but Ollie will send someone."

"One of us needs to talk with Ollie," Hawk said.

"And one of us needs to stick around here," I said. "To greet whoever Ollie sends."

"How 'bout I do that," Hawk said. "Gimme the opportunity to meet the workers."

I nodded.

"And I get to meet Ollie," I said.

"Should be you," Hawk said. "You so charming."

"Yes," I said. "That's certainly true."

"Will you be all right alone?" April said to Hawk.

What she meant of course was *Will we be all right with only one of you on guard?* Hawk knew what she meant. He smiled.

"Be too many of them," Hawk said, "I can always run and hide."

April looked uncertain.

"He's teasing," I said. "Unless you expect to be invaded by China, Hawk will be sufficient."

"You think I not sufficient for China?" Hawk said.

I waffled my hand.

"You might need me for backup," I said.

· 4 ·

Susan came up to her living space from her first-floor office at ten past six in the evening. I was reading the paper and drinking Johnnie Walker Blue on the couch with Pearl. Actually, Pearl was neither reading nor drinking—she was lying on her side with her legs stretched out and her head on my left thigh, making it awkward to turn the page.

Susan said, "Sit right there. Don't disturb the baby."

Pearl wagged her short tail vigorously but didn't get up. Susan came across the living room and kissed me on the mouth, and then kissed Pearl.

"At least I was first," I said.

Susan went to the refrigerator, got out some Riesling, poured some, and sat in the chair opposite me.

"How was today," I said, "in the world of whack jobs?"

"I have a patient for whom love and sex are inextricable," she said. "It makes sex very important and serious and a bit frightening for her."

"And fun?" I said.

"Sadly, no," Susan said. "Not yet. And how is the world of thuggery?"

"April Kyle has resurfaced," I said.

"The little girl you steered into a life of prostitution?"

"I saved her from a life of degrading prostitution and steered her to a life of whoredom with dignity," I said.

"If there is a such," Susan said.

I finished my drink and gathered myself to get up and make another.

"No," Susan said. "I'll get it for you. She's so comfortable."

She made my drink and brought it back.

"There is more dignity and less dignity," I said, "in almost anything."

"I know," Susan said. "I was being playful. You did the best you could with her."

"She was too damaged to become a soccer mom," I said.

"Or a shrink," Susan said. "How is she?"

"She's a grown woman," I said. "It's a little startling. For the last however many years she's been in my memory as a kid, and now she's not a kid."

"Is she still involved in prostitution?"

"In a dignified way," I said.

"Tell me about it," Susan said.

While I was telling, Pearl got up suddenly, as if responding to a voice unheard, and went over and wedged herself up into the wing chair where Susan sat. Pearl weighed seventy-five pounds, which created a territorial issue. Susan resolved it by sliding forward and sitting on the front edge of the chair while Pearl curled up behind her.

"Didn't she begin in some Back Bay home? All that time ago when you first found her?"

"Yeah," I said. "Different location, but, still, back to her roots, I guess."

"She sounds integrated and charming," Susan said.

"She does," I said. "Patricia Utley may have done a good job."

"She cannot have lived the life she's led, especially growing up, without suffering a lot of damage," Susan said.

"I know."

"Under stress," Susan said, "the damage usually surfaces."

"I know."

"You seem to know a lot," Susan said.

"I've been scoring boldly and big-time," I said, "for many years with a really smart shrink."

"Funny," Susan said. "During those moments of bold and big-time scoring, I can't recall that much discussion of the psyche."

"Can you remember any fun?" I said.

"Mostly I just squeeze my eyes tight shut and think of Freud," she said.

I rolled the ice around in my drink for a minute.

"So, do you think prostitution is inevitably demeaning?" I said.

"We are conditioned to think it's demeaning to women," Susan said.

"But not men?"

"We are not conditioned to think it degrades men, I suppose. Though, I suspect, most of us disapprove of men who frequent whores."

"It might degrade both," I said.

"Or maybe we are like my patient," Susan said, "who feels sex has to be a demonstration of love, every time. Maybe we invest it with too much meaning and aren't willing to accept the possibility that sex without love and commitment can still be fun."

"What if there's love and commitment, too?" I said.

"Like us," Susan said. "It probably intensifies everything, but it should be no less fun."

"Chinese food delivered to the house," I said, "is fun."

"Especially when there's love and commitment?"

"Especially then," I said.

"Do I hear you saying you're hungry?"

"Yes."

"What about the question of dignified prostitution?" she said.

"Perhaps over mushu pork," I said. "Or lemon chicken."

"Shall we order in?"

"If I am allowed to eat with a fork," I said. "I hate chopsticks."

"Certainly," Susan said. "If that's fun for you."

I raised my glass to her.

"Scotch and soda," I said, "lemon chicken, and thou."

"I'll make the call," she said.

· 5 ·
_____

Ollie DeMars had space in a small brick building on Southampton Street just before Andrews Square, with its own convenient parking lot. The lot was empty except for somebody's Lexus. I parked beside the Lexus and went into the building.

The room was nearly overwhelmed by a vast television screen on the far wall. Five or six comfortable chairs were arranged in front of the screen, and a couple of hard-looking guys were sitting, watching some sort of program where people ate worms. To my left along the side wall was a big conference table with some straight chairs, and against the wall next to the television, beside a doorway that led further into the building, was a big avocado-colored refrigerator.

One of the men watching reality television turned his head when I came in and said, "You want something?"

"Tank asked me to stop by," I said, "and talk with Ollie."

The man thought about that. He was nearly bald with a really bad comb-over.

"Ollie know you?" he said.

"Only by reputation," I said.

"Reputation," the comb-over guy said.

His viewing partner was bigger than he was, and younger, with dark shoulder-length hair. He turned to look back at me.

"You got a big rep?" Long Hair said.

"Naw," I said. "I'm just your ordinary man of steel. Could you tell Ollie I'm here."

"What if we don't?" Long Hair said.

"Then we may find out about my rep," I said.

It was silly. There was nothing in it for me to get into it with two entry-level street soldiers. But they were annoying me. The long-haired guy got up and stood, looking at me. Then he laughed dismissively and walked through the door beside the refrigerator. Comb-over watched me silently while Long Hair was gone. The time passed quickly.

"Okay, Man of Steel," Long Hair said from the doorway. "Ollie says bring you in."

I followed him down a short corridor and into another room. There was another large television, a desk, and several office-type chairs with arms. There was a phone on the desk, and a computer. On the right-hand wall there was a couch. Behind the desk was a guy who looked like an Ollie. He had sandy hair and a wide, friendly face. When I came in he stood and came around the desk.

"You gotta be Spenser," he said. "I'm Ollie DeMars."

I looked at Long Hair.

"See?" I said. "I told you I had a rep."

He snorted.

"Be okay, Johnny," Ollie said to him. "You can leave us."

Long Hair nodded and went back down the short corridor to his reality show.

"Have a seat," Ollie said.

He had on a blue-checked shirt and a maroon knit tie, and a rust-colored Harris tweed sport coat. He looked like he might sell real estate.

"You've done me a hell of a favor," Ollie said. "I send out guys like Tank and Eddie with the expectation they can get things done."

"Eddie the weight lifter?"

"Yes, and you showed me that they couldn't."

"All part of the service," I said.

"So I canned their ass," he said, and grinned at me like we were pals. "My way or highway, you know?"

"Are you planning to send somebody else?" I said.

He grinned. His teeth seemed unnaturally white.

"Not at these prices," he said. "I gotta deal with you and the schwartza, I need to get paid accordingly."

"Schwartza's name is Hawk," I said. "Who's paying you."

"Tell you the truth," Ollie said, "I don't even know."

"How come you don't know."

"Got a phone call, guy says he wants me to do some work over at a cathouse in the Back Bay. Says have I got a checking account. I say I do. He says he'll wire money to my account. And he does."

"What was the work?"

"Just keep pressuring them until he tells us to stop."

"Pressuring them to do what?"

"Pay up," Ollie said.

"Pay who?" I said.

Ollie shrugged.

"Don't know," he said.

"For what?"

Ollie shook his head.

"Same answer," he said.

"Where'd the wire transfer come from?"

"None of your business," Ollie said.

"Actually, it is," I said.

"Okay," Ollie said. "I still won't tell you."

"Yet," I said.

"Yet?" Ollie said. "Confident bastard, aren't you."

"Optimistic," I said.

"Might want to be a little careful," Ollie said. "I'm fairly optimistic myself."

"Sure," I said. "How's he know you're doing your job? Might be some people who would take the money and do nothing."

"I'm not like that," Ollie said. "I got a reputation."

"You too," I said. "But how does he know?"

Ollie shrugged and shook his head. Multitasking.

"You plan to keep earning the money?"

"I plan to ask for more. I didn't agree to do business with you and Hawk."

"Yet," I said.

Ollie smiled.

"You know Hawk?" I said.

"I been doing this work for a long time," he said. "Of course I know Hawk. Know you, too."

"So you're going to renegotiate," I said.

"Yep."

"How will you get hold of him."

"I'll sit tight until he gets hold of me," Ollie said.

"If you bother April Kyle again," I said, "I'll ruin your life."

Ollie smiled as he spoke. "I said I knew who you were. I didn't say I prayed to you."

He took a silvery semiautomatic pistol out of his desk drawer and pointed it at me sort of informally.

"Could pop you right here, get it done," he said. "But I'm not getting paid to do it, yet."

"So I'm spared," I said.

"Until I renegotiate," Ollie said.

"When you renegotiate," I said, "charge a lot."

Ollie grinned again, still pointing the gun more or less at me. He nodded his head slowly. Then he put the gun down on his desk.

"Well, that fucking terrified you," Ollie said. "Didn't it."

"Iron self-control," I said.

"Attaboy," Ollie said.

· 6 ·

I sat and had coffee with Hawk and April in the front parlor of the mansion. The furniture was men's-club leather. There was a fire in the fireplace. On the walls were reproductions of Picasso's nude sketches.

"You don't know Ollie DeMars," I said.

"No," April said.

"I know Ollie," Hawk said.

"I'm startled," I said.

"Got a crew in Southie," Hawk said. "They steal stuff, hire out to bigger outfits for rough work. Ollie's pretty bad."

"As bad as you?" April said.

Hawk smiled. "Course not," he said.

"And your only contact with Ollie's employer is by anonymous phone call," I said.

"Yes."

"And he wants a percentage of your operation."

"Twenty-five percent," April said.

"How does he know how much that would be?" I said.

"I don't know."

"How much would it be?" I said.

"All of my markup," she said.

"You have a lot of overhead," I said.

"This is not a half-hour in a cheap hotel," April said.

I nodded. Hawk sipped his coffee. He was expressionless. And, except for drinking the coffee, he was motionless. It was as if nothing interested him, as if he saw nothing and heard nothing. Except that later, if it mattered, it would turn out that he had seen and heard everything.

"How do you suppose he knows about you?" I said.

"Maybe he was a customer," April said.

"Or is," Hawk said.

April looked startled, and then uneasy.

"You think he might still be coming here?" she said.

"No way to know," I said. "How do people find you?"

"Most of it is referral," April said.

"Satisfied customers?"

"Yes."

"And how did they get to you?" I said.

"We have some contacts in good hotels, limousine services, some of the big travel agencies. And of course there's the Internet."

"The Internet," I said.

"Look up 'escort services' on one of the search engines," April said.

Hawk said, "I explain to you later what a search engine is."

"No need for scorn," I said. "I have a cell phone, too."

"Ever use it?" Hawk said.

"I'm thinking about it," I said. "What will I find under escort services."

"About three million hits," April said. "Nationwide."

"So if I'm going to, say, Pittsburgh," I said, "I look up escort services in Pittsburgh and there's a list."

"A big list," April said.

"And that's true of Boston?"

"Heavens," April said, "that's true of Stockton, California."

"And you're listed in Boston?"

"Sure," April said. "And about two hundred thousand others. We feel that it's in our best interest to put our name in play. But we don't rely on the Internet, and we screen the Internet customers very carefully."

"What are you screening for?"

"We are looking for repeat business," she said. "We want grown-ups who value discretion and top-drawer accommodations. We are looking for people who travel first-class."

"How can you tell?" I said.

"One learns," she said and smiled.

"I show up, they let me in," Hawk said to me. "You show up, they don't."

"Hawk," April said, "we probably wouldn't even charge you."

"So this guy could be a local customer, or somebody who found you on the Internet," I said. "He could, I suppose, be one of the people that shill for you."

April hunched her shoulders as if the room were cold.

"I don't like to think that," she said. "And I don't like to call them shills."

"Sorry," I said. "How about referral associates."

She smiled.

"Better," she said.

"Could be more than just April," Hawk said.

"Maybe," I said. "Either way, it needs to be somebody that would know how to find Ollie DeMars. Ollie probably doesn't have a website."

"So we looking for someone can find the right whorehouse—excuse me, April—and the right enforcer."

"Most people wouldn't know, either," I said.

Hawk nodded. We were quiet for a minute. Then, just as I said, "Cop," Hawk began to nod his head.

"A cop?" April said.

"Local, state, federal, any cop." I said. "Any cop can easily come up with a story that would get him this information, and no one would question it."

"Federal?" April said. "You mean it could be, like, an FBI agent?"

"Sure," I said. "Or California Highway Patrol, or a U.S. Marshal, or a precinct commander in Chicago, or some Sheriff's Deputy in Cumberland County."

"Where's Cumberland County," April said.

Susan did that, too, asked questions out on the periphery of what I was saying. I wondered if it was a female trait . . . or did I obfuscate . . . female trait sounded right.

"Maine," I said. "Around Portland."

"Maybe you scared him off," April said.

"We'll see," I said. "Until we know, Hawk or I will hang around here."

"I the thug," Hawk said. "You the sleuth. I do the hanging around. You sleuth us up something."

"You want to go pack a bag or something?" I said.

"Keep a bag in my car," Hawk said. "So I got clothes and ammunition. One of the young ladies on staff went out and bought me the new Thomas Friedman book."

"And you expect to get paid for this?" I said to Hawk.

"Half what you get," Hawk said. "Like always."

"This one may be pro bono," I said.

"Sure," Hawk said, "long as you split it with me."

· 7 ·

I stood at my office window and looked down at Berkeley Street. It had snowed often in January, and the streets were compressed by snowbanks. Sidewalks were difficult, and the plows further snarled the already encumbered traffic. Still, the sun was bright, and some of the young women from the big insurance offices were out for early lunch.

Outside the bank below my office, at the corner of Boylston, a big Cadillac SUV pulled over. Ty-Bop got out of the backseat and opened the front door. Tony Marcus, in a tweed overcoat with a fur collar, stepped out and picked his way across a snowbank toward my building. The Cadillac pulled away. Junior was probably driving, if the SUV was big enough.

I was behind my desk by the time they got to my office. I had the side drawer open, where I kept a spare piece. Ty-Bop opened the door and Tony walked through.

He said, "Spenser."

I said, "Tony."

Tony hung his coat up carefully, and pulled up a chair and sat, hiking his pant legs to protect the creases. Ty-Bop lingered by the door with his hat on sideways over cornrows. He was wearing droopy jeans and a thigh-length, too-big, unbuttoned Philadelphia 76ers warm-up jacket over some sort of football jersey. He looked about twenty, a standard gangsta rap fan in funny clothes, except he could put a bullet in your eye from fifty yards. Either eye.

"How's the family?" I said to Tony.

Tony shrugged.

"Your son-in-law is no longer in Marshport, I assume."

"We both knew he wouldn't be," Tony said.

"Daughter okay?"

"No worse," Tony said.

I nodded.

"You give my son-in-law a break in Marshport," Tony said.

"No reason not to," I said.

Tony nodded. "What's your problem with Ollie DeMars?" he said.

"Couple of his crew were bothering a woman I know," I said. "Hawk and I asked them to stop."

"April Kyle," Tony said.

I nodded.

"Ollie not somebody to let that slide," Tony said.

"He tells me he's just an employee on this, and is waiting instructions from his employer."

"He say who he employer is?" Tony said.

"Says he doesn't know."

Tony frowned. I continued.

"Says he gets his instructions by anonymous phone call. Says he gets paid by anonymous wire transfer."

"How do you get anonymous wire transfers?" Tony said.

"Ollie declined to comment," I said.

"Offshore account, maybe," Tony said.

"Maybe," I said.

Tony leaned back in his chair and put his fingertips together in a kind of tent in front of his chest. He was a medium-size black man with a soft-looking neck, a modest Afro, and a thick mustache. His clothes probably cost more than several cars I'd driven. He looked prosperous and soft. He was more than prosperous. But he wasn't soft. Like Hawk, he moved easily in and out of black-speak as it suited him.

"They is a couple approaches to the whore business," he said. "There's volume—a bunch of hookers, ten, twelve johns a day. And then there's quality-not-quantity. One daily fee."

"But a big one," I said.

Tony nodded.

"As you know," he said, "I have always felt that whores are a black business."

"I love racial pride," I said.

Tony smiled.

"Without his heritage," Tony said, "what's a man got?"

"Money," I said. "Power. Women, scotch whiskey, Ty-Bop to shoot anyone you don't like. Cars, clothes, guns . . ."

Tony smiled and put up a hand.

"Okay, so maybe heritage ain't everything," he said.

"Maybe running half the city is something," I said.

"But it's only half," Tony said.

"So far," I said. "And heritage has nothing to do with it."

"I pretty well got all the whoring organized in this city," Tony said. "I got a tight hand on the volume end of it, but the blue-blood part of the business is labor-intensive, ties up a lot of capital, so I let the blue bloods run it and take a franchising fee."

I nodded. I looked at Ty-Bop leaning against the wall next to the door. In my experience, Ty-Bop rarely spoke. He was rocking gently to the sound of music no one else was hearing. There was no sign that he heard anything being said.

"You collect from April?" I said.

"Sure. She'll tell you that. Price of doing business," Tony said. "But not so much that they can't make a profit. I want them in business."

"And if they don't pay?"

"Send somebody over," Tony said.

"And if Hawk and I show up?"

"Maybe send more people," Tony said. "But it ain't relevant anyway. She always pay."

I waited. Tony looked at his tented fingers. Ty-Bop continued rocking to the music of the spheres.

"Now there seem to be somebody else in the woodpile," Tony said.

"Nice metaphor," I said.

Tony shrugged. "Ain't no room for two of us," he said.

"And you figure I might be looking for him, too."

"Uh-huh."

"He trying to cut in on other places besides April?" I said.

"Somebody is."

"Ollie doing the muscle work?"

"Yeah."

"And you haven't intervened?" I said.

"Not yet," Tony said. "Ollie's a tough nut to crack. We crack it if we have to. But you eliminate Ollie and another Ollie will turn up. It ain't efficient."

"But eliminate his employer and you won't have to eliminate Ollie," I said.

"Tha's right," Tony said.

"You believe Ollie," I said. "That he doesn't know?"

"Don't know," Tony said. "Was hoping you might shed some light."

"You don't think it's Ollie himself?" I said.

"His crew does mostly muscle work," Tony said. "Ollie ain't a whore-business guy."

"You think the employer is local?" I said.

Tony put his fingertips against his lips and tapped them lightly as he thought about the question.

"Never thought he wasn't," Tony said after a while.

"So," I said. "We're teaming up to crack the case?"

"Thought I'd let you know I was interested," Tony said. "You find this guy, might be something in it for you."

"What might be in it for him?" I said.

"You wouldn't need to worry 'bout that," Tony said.

"Nice," I said.

Tony stood and put on his coat. Outside my window the snow was starting to come down again. Small flakes, not falling hard but falling quite steady.

"We got a common interest here, Spenser," Tony said.

"I know," I said. "I'll keep you on the mailing list."

"Good," Tony said.

He nodded at Ty-Bop. Ty-Bop took out a cell phone and dialed and said something I couldn't hear. Then he opened the door and went out. Tony went out behind him. I went to my window and looked down at Berkeley Street. The Caddy SUV pulled up. Ty-Bop opened the front door. Tony got in. Ty-Bop closed the front door and got in the back. The Caddy pulled away across Boylston, straight on down Berkeley toward the river.

I closed my desk drawer.

·8·

There is a walkway down the center of the mall on Commonwealth Avenue, and the city had kept it shoveled during the winter. They hadn't yet gotten to it this snowfall, and there was maybe an inch of dry snow beneath our feet as April and I walked down toward the Public Garden in the early evening. The snowfall had slowed to a light haze that created halos on the streetlights and made the expensive condos in their handsome brownstone look especially comfortable.

"You've not heard from the anonymous caller," I said.

"No."

"Business is okay?" I said. "Hawk isn't scaring the clients?"

"Business is as good as ever," April said. "Hawk has stayed pretty much in the background, and there haven't been any incidents."

The evening commuter traffic in this part of town was on Storrow Drive and the Pike. The traffic moving on Commonwealth was mostly cabs. The only other pedestrians on the mall were people with dogs.

"So," I said, "since I last saw you . . ."

"You mean when I was still a kid?"

"Yeah."

"After I left you and Susan, I went back to Mrs. Utley, in New York, and . . . she sort of brought me up."

"You worked for her," I said.

"Yes. She taught me how to dress, how to walk, how to speak. She showed me how to order in good restaurants."

"She did a lot of that before you ran off with Rambeaux," I said.

"My God, you remember his name."

"I do," I said.

"She taught me to read books, and go to shows, and follow the newspaper so I could talk intelligently. I still read *The New York Times* every morning."

"Any love interests since Rambeaux?"

"No," April said. "And she always gave me the best assignments. No creepy stuff—young men, mostly. Regular customers."

"But none you've met that matter to you."

"Oh God, you're still such a romantic," she said. "Whores don't fall in love. I learned that from Rambeaux."

"He was the wrong guy to fall in love with," I said. "Doesn't mean there isn't a right one."

She laughed. I heard no humor in the sound.

"Men are pigs," she said.

"Oink," I said.

"Except you."

"There may be another one someplace that isn't," I said. "I'm not even absolutely sure Hawk is or isn't."

She sighed loudly.

"*Most* men are pigs, okay?" she said.

"So what's your social life?" I said.

"Social life?"

"Yeah."

"I don't have much of a social life," she said. "Mostly I work."

"Friends?"

"I get along well with my employees," she said.

"Any free time?" I said.

"If I have free time I go to the gym. How I look matters in my work."

"Turn tricks anymore?" I said.

"Now and then, for fun, with the right guy."

"What would make him right?"

"He'd need to be interested in someone my age, for one thing."

"Anything else?" I said. "That would make him right?"

"Oh, leave me the hell alone," April said. "I almost forget what you're like. You're still working on me."

"Working on you?" I said.

"You're still trying to save me, for crissake. This is what I am. You can't save me."

"Except maybe from the anonymous caller," I said.

We paused at Clarendon Street and waited for the light.

"I guess I earned that," she said. "I came to you for help. But couldn't you just help me with that?"

"Sure," I said.

· 9 ·

"You know something that occurred to me," I said to Susan.

"I know what usually occurs to you," she said.

"Besides that," I said. "Men, at least straight men, have no idea what other men are like during sex."

"Are you planning to ask me?"

"No," I said. "But presumably, conversely, straight women probably have very little idea what other women are like during sex."

"Are you planning to tell me?"

"No."

"Isn't it swell that it occurred to you," Susan said.

"You're not interested?"

"No."

We were sharing a Cuban sandwich at the bar in Chez Henri. Susan felt that Riesling was appropriate with a Cuban sandwich. I was drinking beer.

"Men think about stuff like that," I said.

"Women don't," Susan said.

"Are we both generalizing from our own experiences?" I said.

"Yes," Susan said.

"April says all men are pigs," I said.

"Her experience may have contributed to that view," Susan said.

"Sure," I said. "But I have no way to know. Is it certain that the men she has encountered are pigs?"

"Not everyone patronizes whores," Susan said.

"And those who do so regularly," I said, "maybe have something wrong with them."

Susan nodded. She had cut a small wedge of one half of the sandwich and was chewing a small bite she had taken.

"I don't find you unduly piggish," she said.

"Wow," I said. "Thanks for the vote of confidence."

She smiled and sipped her wine. "Why are you so interested?" she said.

"I worry about April," I said.

"Probably with reason," Susan said.

"She seems so integrated, and calm," I said. "It's kind of heartwarming. And then we're walking along and I ask about her social life, and she says all men are pigs."

"Including you?"

"When I raised that issue, she said *except me*."

"If I may generalize," Susan said, "everyone general-izes. We just got through generalizing, you may recall."

"But this generalization seems to have cut her off from any possibility of . . . love?"

"She has spent her life in circumstances where love was a commercial exchange," Susan said. "As I recall the time when she got into the biggest trouble, where you had to in a sense buy her back, she did so out of love."

"You think that was love?" I said.

"She thought it was. It didn't make her more likely to feel love again."

I ate some sandwich and drank some beer.

"When I was about twenty-two," I said, "I went with two other guys to Japan on R & R. We stayed in a hotel near the Sugamo subway stop, with some girls we had rented for the week. We took hot baths, and they cooked us food on a hibachi in the room, first time I ever had sukiyaki, and we had what seemed at the time reasonable sex in reasonable amounts. It was very pleasant. After a week we went back to war."

"Your point?" Susan said.

I could feel her eyes on me. She was becoming inter-ested. The force of her interest was always tangible.

"We liked each other. We weren't contemptuous of them. Maybe if we were, the language barrier made it easier to hide, but I felt no disdain. We didn't feel anything for them, either. We were sort of like new pals, having some fun . . . for a short while."

Susan nodded.

"Yes," she said.

"It was the last time I was with a prostitute."

"Probably drank some during that week, too," Susan said.

"Absolutely."

"War, whiskey, and women," Susan said.

"The big three," I said.

"Can you say rites of passage?"

"I know," I said. "And it may look more charming in that context."

"So where are you going with this?" Susan said.

"I don't know. It's bothering me."

"April is better off than she would have been," Susan said, "if she hadn't met you."

"Yes," I said. "I think that's so. But it doesn't mean she's well off."

"That's true," Susan said. "It is also true that you are not God."

"You don't know that," I said.

Susan smiled at me with her eyes while she took another delicate bite of the small wedge she had cut off her half of the Cuban sandwich.

"After I talked with April the other night," I said, "I went home and looked up escort services on the Web. She's right, there's millions of listings. And pretty soon, as you would expect, they linked to porn sites. So I surfed the porn sites. I didn't sign up, I just looked at the marketing."

"And you always read *Playboy* for the articles," Susan said.

"Scan a few porn sites," I said. "After a short time, they become pretty repellent. What struck me was the contempt with which the product is marketed. It seems aimed almost entirely at people who dislike women. The women are always referred to as whores or sluts or bitches or whatever. They are voraciously eager to dangle your doop or flap your floop or whatever the site was selling. I even scanned some gay sites. Same thing. The object of desire, male or female, is treated with scorn, except for their uncontrollable willingness to bleep your bippy."

"No mutuality," Susan said.

"None," I said.

"You're not the first to notice that," Susan said.

"How disappointing," I said.

Susan smiled. "So you're saying commercial sex and porn dehumanize the object of desire?"

"And the object which desires," I said. "Works both ways."

"So perhaps pornography and prostitution are not victimless crimes," Susan said.

"Probably not," I said. "The trick is to figure out which is the victim."

"The questions are too cosmic for me," Susan said. "But on a level where I can operate, it seems clear that April, while perhaps less unfortunate than she was, is still a victim."

·10·

One of April's girls, on her night off, was walking back from Copley Place when she was yanked into an alley near the mansion and badly beaten. Her nose was broken; a tooth was knocked out. Her face was bruised and a rib was cracked. She was out for a while and when she came to, she got herself up and dragged herself back to the mansion, where April called an ambulance.

They set her nose and taped her ribs and gave her some pain meds and kept her overnight for observation. In the morning, April and I brought her home.

"You take as much time as you need, Bev," April said. "Get better."

Bev tried a small smile, but it fell short.

"Nobody's paying anything for me the way I look now."

"You'll be fine once you recover," April said. "You need dental work, we'll get it for you."

Bev tried a nod, and that hurt, too, so she didn't do anything.

"Don't be afraid of the Percocet," I said. "Take it as scheduled, even if you don't need it."

"You ever get beat up?" Bev said.

"Some," I said. "It's important to stay ahead of the pain."

April went upstairs with her. I went in the living room with Hawk.

"So do I walk them to the movies now?" he said.

"And while you're gone they bust in here and make a mess?" I said.

"Be a good plan," Hawk said.

I nodded.

"Beating her up could have been a random act."

"Sure it could," Hawk said.

"But we both know it's not," I said.

"Course we do," Hawk said.

"Making trouble here is much more effective," I said. "It'll ruin her business overnight."

"But I'm here," Hawk said.

"So they beat this kid up," I said. "Maybe to see if that will scare April into doing what they want, maybe in hopes you'll start escorting the girls outside, and they can come here unimpeded."

"Maybe both," Hawk said.

"We need to impede both," I said.

"We a body or two short," Hawk said.

"Maybe we should call Vinnie," I said.

"Outta town," Hawk said. "Gino's opening up something in Cincinnati. Vinnie supporting his efforts."

"How long?"

"Vinnie thinks he'll be a while," Hawk said. "He got a lot of people to persuade."

"Well, he's not the only thug we know."

"How about the little pachuco from LA," Hawk said.

"Pachuco?" I said. "Nobody says pachuco anymore."

"Or the tough fag from Georgia," Hawk said.

"Tedy Sapp?" I said. "You think he calls you the tough nigger from Boston?"

"Probably," Hawk said. "Toughest fag I ever saw."

"I'll make the calls," I said.

· 11 ·

I talked to Chollo first.

"You know what a pachuco is," I said.

"I used to."

"Hawk thinks you're a pachuco," I said.

"We all pachucos at heart, Señor," Chollo said.

"*Sí,*" I said. "You want to come to Boston?"

"Where it's eight degrees with thirty inches of snow," Chollo said.

"I need some backup."

"Mr. Del Rio is in conflict with some gentlemen from my native land," Chollo said, "and I'm supposed to go down there with Bobby Horse and resolve it."

"In the usual way?" I said.

"*Sí.*"

"Take a while?" I said.

"Not after we find them," Chollo said. "How 'bout Vinnie?"

"He's doing something in Cincinnati," I said.

"Didn't know anybody was doing something in Cincinnati," Chollo said.

"I've had fun in Cincinnati," I said.

"Gringos have fun in Pasadena," Chollo said. "I'm sorry I can't help you out, my friend."

"Okay," I said. "Walk careful in Mexico."

"I am as stealthy as a Mexican jaguar," he said.

"I didn't know they had jaguars in Mexico," I said.

"I think they don't," Chollo said. "But if they did, that's how stealthy I would be."

We hung up and I dialed Tedy Sapp. He was where he usually was, at the Bathhouse Bar and Grill in Lamarr, Georgia.

"I need some help up here," I said, "in Massachusetts, the only state that permits gay marriage."

"Nice neutral presentation," Sapp said. "Whaddya need."

I told him.

"What's it pay?" he said.

"Haven't established a price yet."

"How's the weather up there?"

"It's up to fifteen today, thirty inches of snow. No wind."

"Will I be in danger of getting shot?"

"Some," I said.

"Perfect," Sapp said. "You want me right away?"

"Tomorrow would be good."

"Okay," Tedy said. "Can you provide me a piece when I get there?"

"Sure," I said.

"So it's freezing and snowy and I might get shot and the pay is uncertain, but you will provide me a weapon, and if I want to marry somebody up there, I can, and it'll be legal."

"Long as you stay here," I said.

"A gay boy's dream," he said. "See you tomorrow."

· 12 ·

April and I were having coffee and watching Hawk play chess with Tedy Sapp in the front room at the mansion. They had been through a small war together out west a few years back, and, within the limits of each man's emotional range, they liked each other. In some ways they were the exact opposite. Black, white. Straight, gay. But at the core they were almost the same guy. They were smart. Their word was good. They were fearsome. And they knew it. They were both certain that they could kick any ass in the world, and it gave them a kind of ironic serenity . . . even though I might wish to add a small disclaimer to the premise.

"Bev is quitting," April said.

I nodded.

"A lot of the girls are talking about quitting," she said.

"We can protect them," I said. "But . . ."

"It will put me out of business if many of them quit," April said. She wore a black cashmere sweater with a V-neck and jeans.

"Recruiting is not easy. I can't just go buy ten surplus hookers from some pimp. These girls aren't really professional prostitutes."

"Isn't *amateur prostitute* some sort of oxymoron," I said.

"This is not like other places," April said. "I have graduate students. I have teachers; I have housewives whose husbands travel. I have a flight attendant. I have a woman who sells real estate. These are women of substance."

"And they do this why?"

April shrugged.

"They like money. They like sex. They like adventure. They get a lot of money for doing what they have often done for nothing."

"Where do you find them?" I said.

"You don't have to find many. Once you start, it becomes sort of networking," April said. "But we begin by, say, answering personal ads on the Internet or in reputable publications. We send them a discreet query. Would you be interested in escort work? Or we send someone out to dating bars, pick up the right-looking woman, ask the same discreet thing."

"Eliminate those who are not . . . *our kind*?"

"Don't laugh at me," she said. "This is not a bunch of sweaty people grunting in the dark. This is a first-class private club. I want my girls to enjoy sex. I want my clients to be with girls who enjoy sex."

"The real deal," I said.

"Exactly. That's just the right phrase. This is the real deal."

"So why don't your clients just go and avail themselves of women like this for nothing. They are there."

"Because it's troublesome. Because they would have to go through the screening process that we go through for them. We screen very carefully."

"You do that?"

"Yes," April said. "Men come here knowing they'll have an affectionate, sexy time with attractive, intelligent, and well-spoken women."

"AIDS?" I said.

"That risk exists in any sexual encounter," April said, "unless it's a long-term monogamous one. Short of that, we take every precaution. Our girls are regularly tested. Our clients are from a level of society that is less likely to encounter AIDS."

"And the personal services?" I said.

"Well, aren't you nosy," she said.

"Part of my profession," I said. "I can withdraw the question."

"Sometimes, special circumstances."

"I think I won't explore the special circumstances," I said.

She shrugged.

"No big deal," she said. "Sometimes a client wants to fuck the boss."

"The house mother, so to speak."

April stared at me. "Are you being shrinky with me?" she said.

"Just a thought," I said.

"Well, I know you're with Susan and all, but I don't buy any of that."

"I'm not selling it," I said.

"Sorry," April said. "I've just . . . I tried it for a while. . . . Most of the shrinks I talked with were crazier than I was."

We were quiet. Tedy picked up a chess piece and moved it. Hawk studied the move. Their concentration was palpable.

"Do you play chess?" April said.

"No," I said.

"Do you know how?"

"No."

"I don't either," she said.

Hawk picked up his chess piece and moved it. Tedy nodded slowly as if he approved.

"Could you come to my office with me for a moment?" April said.

"Sure."

We left the room and walked past the concierge and down the hall to the office. The office staff was busy at their computers.

"Tell me a little more about Tedy Sapp," she said.

"What more?" I said.

"He seems, sort of, different."

"He is different," I said. "So is Hawk. So am I. We're all different. It's why we do what we do."

"But . . . what's going on with the hair?"

"Too blond?" I said.

"And artificial. He looks like some sort of ridiculous wrestler or bodybuilder or something."

"Tedy's gay," I said. "He fought it for a long time. The bright hair is sort of a statement: *I'm not trying to pass.*"

"But can he really do what he's supposed to?"

I was quiet for a moment. There were a lot of things to say. But I didn't say any of them. I just answered the question.

"Better than almost anyone," I said.

· 13 ·

I was at my desk, with my feet up, on the phone with Patricia Utley, who was at home in New York. Pearl was spending quality time with me, in my office, on her couch, lying upside down with her head hanging and her tongue lolling. She seemed boneless lying there, and nerveless, as if time and stress were of no consequence and eternity were a plaything.

"When you brought her to me she was a terrified child," Patricia Utley was saying. "I cleaned her up and began to train her. I didn't send her out for a year."

"Orphans of the Storm," I said.

"Well, not entirely, I am a businesswoman. But my childhood was somewhat turbulent, and I was sympathetic."

"And you're maybe softer than you pretend," I said.

"You would understand that," she said. "She was nearly grown and making good progress when she ran off with that idiot Rambeaux."

"Who was not softer than he pretended."

"Hardly," Patricia Utley said.

"Give all for love," I said.

"Give something for love, perhaps. Not everything," Patricia Utley said. "By the time you got her back to me I had to start nearly all over with her."

"She'd had a bad time," I said.

"Many people do," Patricia Utley said. "Especially in the whore business. We try to be the exception."

"We all try," I said. "You succeeded."

"Is that your imitation of Humphrey Bogart?"

"How good is it if you have to ask?" I said.

"Think about it," Patricia Utley said. "Eventually, we got April back on her feet and she became one of my most successful girls."

"So what about this business you set her up in?" I said.

"It's not a wonderful business. But it gives her a chance to run her own show and make a decent living. I did it mainly for April."

"You take back a royalty?"

"Yes. Ten percent."

"Of the gross?" I said.

"Of the net," she said.

"You are doing this," I said, "for April."

"Yes, my take is little more than seven thousand five hundred dollars a year."

"So the business is worth about seventy-five thousand dollars to April."

"Roughly," Patricia Utley said. "There is a lot of overhead."

"The house, the furnishings, the working girls, the office staff," I said.

"And the bar and dining room, and bribes to law enforcement, payment to Mr. Marcus, cleaning services, quite a large laundry bill, physical exams for the girls, clothing allowances."

"Pay the girls' salaries?" I said.

"The whores? They get an advance against earnings. If, in a relatively short time, they don't earn out, they are outplaced."

"How's it compare with your operation in New York," I said.

"For profit?"

"Yes."

"Pocket change," she said. "There's too little volume, too much overhead. I may never get my investment back."

"Has it got an upside down the road?"

"No," Patricia Utley said. "I doubt it. I have not hovered over this project, but it seems that it has as large a share of the market as it is likely to get."

Pearl got off the couch suddenly and walked swiftly around my office until she found a dirty and badly tattered stuffed toy animal of indeterminate species. She picked it up and chewed on it so it squeaked and brought it to me.

"What on earth is that noise?" Patricia Utley said.

"Squeaky toy," I said.

Pearl squeaked it at me some more until I took it and tossed it across the room.

"Have you ever worried that maybe you are alone too much," Patricia Utley said.

"Susan and I have a dog," I said, "and she's come to work today with Daddy."

"My God," Patricia Utley said.

Pearl picked up her squeaky toy and shook it and looked at me, and made a decision, and jumped up on the couch with her squeaky toy and lay down with it underneath her.

"Are you going to tell me why you called," Patricia Utley said.

"Someone's trying to shake April down."

"And she came to you."

"Yes."

"Do you know who it is?"

"Not yet," I said.

"Do you have any help?" she said.

"Two men."

"So there will be some cost," she said.

"Some."

"Has April paid you?"

"No."

"She probably can't really afford to," Patricia Utley said. "When it's done, if you'll submit me a bill, perhaps I will pay you."

"Let's revisit the question when it's done," I said.

"Do you need any other help?" Patricia Utley said. "Stephen is gone. But I have resources."

"I'm fine," I said. "Sorry to hear about Stephen."

"We were together a long time," she said.

"Not long enough," I said.

"It's never long enough," she said. "Is it."

· 14 ·

It was an ironclad rule at Susan's house that Pearl did not eat supper before five p.m.

"If you give in to her," Susan always said, "we'll be feeding her supper at noon."

This was perfectly true, and the rule made a great deal of sense. So after Pearl and I walked the four blocks back to my place in the late afternoon, I ignored her insistent stare unshakably, and didn't feed her until 4:11.

Pearl was an efficient and focused eater. By 4:13 her dish was empty and she was topping it off with a long lap at her water dish. Then, having fulfilled her responsibilities for the day, she got up on the couch and curled up and looked at me. Susan was at a conference in Albany and wouldn't be back until tomorrow. I was in for the night. I went to my kitchen counter and made myself a drink and brought it to the couch and sat down beside

Pearl. It was a tall drink, scotch with soda and a lot of ice. It had a nice, clean look to it. I drank some. It tasted like it looked. I patted Pearl.

The room was so familiar that I barely saw it. I'd been here a long time. I had first had sex with Susan in this room, on a couch not unlike this one. I would have hung on to it for sentimental reasons, maybe with a plaque. But Susan is very big on out with the old and in with the new, and it had been replaced. I got something out of it, though. We'd had sex on this couch, too. If Pearl knew that, she wasn't impressed by it. She was asleep and snoring very faintly. I sipped my drink. Pacing is important. I was never happy when Susan was away. I didn't need to see her every day. We were careful about that. Neither of us wished to be an obligation. But I liked it better when she was nearby and if I wanted to see her, I could. Even if I didn't.

I looked across the living room at the darkness outside my front window. It was the beginning of February. Football was almost over. Baseball hadn't started. Basketball was boring until the last two minutes. And the snow remained deep, dirty, and unmelting. Seven weeks to spring equinox. My drink was gone. I got up carefully, not to disturb Pearl, and made myself a fresh one. I took it back to the couch, sat back down carefully, put my feet on the coffee table, and took a swallow. Winter would pass. Pearl shifted a little in her sleep, and I shifted a little to accommodate her. . . . There was something really wrong with April's story.

From the start, I had felt vaguely uncomfortable. I didn't know what I was uncomfortable about. And, suddenly, I did. The mansion-class prostitution business she was running wasn't worth the energy someone was expending to get a cut of it. If Patricia Utley was right— and if she wasn't, who would be?—the business was labor-intensive, difficult to run, and generated a modest profit. Was the business worth getting involved with Ollie DeMars? Was it worth inviting trouble with Tony Marcus? Or, for that matter, me and Hawk? And who was it that they dispatched to dating bars to pick up women and recruit them? Wouldn't that have to be a guy? What guy? Of course Patricia Utley could be lying. But why would she be?

"Moreover," I said to Pearl, "since the tactics of the anonymous takeover seem aimed at putting April out of business, what will the takeover guy have if his tactics work?"

Pearl appeared disinterested.

I felt bad about April. She was lying, and that made helping her a lot harder. Plus, what could be so bad that she wouldn't tell me?

"And," I said to Pearl, "the ugly truth of the matter is, my feelings are hurt."

Pearl opened her eyes for a moment and stared at me. I took another swallow of scotch and looked back at her.

"Okay," I said. "I'll get over it."

Pearl closed her eyes.

· 15 ·

In the morning Pearl and I took a short run along the river. The footing was bad, and the wind off the river was irksome. But we got in a half-hour of running plus some loitering while Pearl performed her morning ablutions and I, responsible dog owner, cleaned up after her. It is hard to look graceful while being a responsible dog owner. But I felt I managed with considerable aplomb. We went back to my place through the back basement door of my building. I fed Pearl and got some coffee and went and stood and looked down at Marlboro Street while I drank it. I always stood at the window while I had my coffee. I liked to watch the people going to work. A gray Ford Crown Victoria with tinted windows pulled onto Marlboro Street from Arlington and slid into a space by a hydrant across the street from my building. No one got out. The car was idling; I could see the exhaust plume drifting up behind the car. I drank some more coffee and stayed at the window. No one got out of the car. A man walking a small Jack Russell terrier went by. A woman in a short faux-fur coat and tight slacks went by. The Crown Vic did not have LV plates, so it probably wasn't a limo waiting to take someone to Logan Airport. I watched it some more. It sat. I drank coffee. My cup was empty. I got another cup. The Crown Vic still sat there, still idling. So they could run the heater. While I watched the Crown Vic, the window on the passenger side slid down and somebody tossed a foam coffee cup and a couple of napkins onto Marlboro Street. I could see that he had long hair. I recognized him. He had been in Ollie DeMars's office when I had gone to visit.

"By God," I said to Pearl, "a clue!"

Pearl raised her head from the couch and looked at me closely to make sure I hadn't said, "Do you want something to eat." When she established that I hadn't, she put her head back down. I continued on my coffee. The Crown Vic continued to sit. I got my cordless phone and brought it to the window and dialed the mansion and talked with Tedy Sapp.

"I'm looking out the front window of my apartment," I said. "There is a gray Crown Vic parked across the street and in it are several guys who bear me ill will."

"You must see that a lot," Sapp said. "Given how charming you are."

"Hawk needs to stay with April," I said. "But he will tell you how to get here."

"Okay."

"Here's what I want you to do," I said.

Tedy listened while I told him. He didn't interrupt me. He didn't ask any questions.

When I got through, he said, "How long a walk?"

"Fifteen minutes," I said.

"See you there," he said and hung up.

I was still in running shoes and sweats. I went to the front hall closet where I kept my guns, and unlocked it. I put my short .38 up on the shelf and took down my Browning 9mm. I didn't know how many people were in the car. I might want more than five rounds. The magazine was already in the Browning. I jacked a shell up into the chamber, and eased the hammer back down and locked the closet. Then I got my official 2004 Red Sox World Series Championship hat. I put it on and a sheepskin coat. I put the Browning on my hip. Then I checked the time, gave Pearl a kiss on her nose, and went out. I stood on my front steps for a time, savoring the morning. I saw Tedy Sapp walking down Marlboro from the other end. I smiled to myself. He was wearing a peacoat and no hat and his ridiculous blond hair shone in the winter sun. He moved so easily, it was easy not to notice how big he was.

· 16 ·

When Tedy got close enough so that the timing would be right, I went down the stairs and started up Marlboro toward Berkeley. I had my hands in my coat pockets. I was whistling happily. Looking for love and feeling groovy. When I was far enough from my building so that I couldn't dash back inside, four guys got out of the Crown Vic and walked across the street toward me. One of them was Long Hair; beside him was the guy with the comb-over. With them was a blocky guy in a Patriots jacket, and a guy with a shaved head and tattoos on his neck. I stopped when they got to me.

"White guys look like shit with their heads shaved," I said to the group in general.

The guy with the shaved head said, "You talking about me, pal?"

"Just a general observation," I said.

"Never mind that crap," Comb-over said. "Got a message to deliver from Ollie DeMars."

"Wow," I said, "a message."

Long Hair and Comb-over were in front of me. The other two had moved behind me. One of them, it was the guy with the Patriots jacket, tried to put his arms around me and pin my arms. I turned sideways before he could get me pinned and hit him on the side of the face with my elbow. He let go and staggered backward as Tedy Sapp arrived behind Long Hair and Comb-over. Sapp hit Long Hair across the back of the head with his forearm. It knocked Long Hair face forward into the salt slush of the sidewalk. I hit Baldy four times as fast as I could punch. Straight left, left hook, left hook, right cross. He went down. I turned to look for the guy in the Patriots jacket. He was backing away. I looked at Comb-over. He was trying to get a gun out from inside his coat. When it was out, Tedy Sapp chopped it from his hand, almost contemptuously. Comb-over backed up a step with his hands raised in front of him. Sapp kicked him in the groin hard enough to lift him from the ground. Comb-over yelped and fell forward, doubled over in pain, and lay in the slush. Sapp and I both looked at the guy in the Patriots jacket. He backed up another couple of steps and then turned and ran. We watched him until he turned right on Arlington and disappeared.

I looked at the three men on the ground. Comb-over would take a while to recover. Baldy was on his hands and knees with his head hanging. Long Hair was sitting up. We did a fast shakedown to make sure there were no other weapons. There weren't.

"I love the pat-down part," Sapp said.

"Pervert," I said.

"Your point?" Sapp said.

I grinned.

"Since they had four guys and one gun," I said, "I'd guess they weren't going to pop me."

Sapp nodded.

"What was the message?" I said to Long Hair.

He looked at the sidewalk and shook his head.

"Now that's dumb," I said. "You just got your ass handed to you by a couple of guys who could spend the week doing it again if they had reason. What did Ollie want you to tell me?"

Sapp poked Long Hair in the ribs gently with the toe of his work boot. Long Hair looked at him, and then at me.

"Ollie says to tell you to stay away from the whores."

"And?"

"And give you a good beatin'," Long Hair said.

"Well," I said. "You did your best."

We were quiet. No sirens wailed in the distance. No patrol cars pulled around the corner from Arlington Street. If anyone had seen the fight, they hadn't thought enough about it to call the cops. I looked at Long Hair. He didn't know anything. None of them did. They were street labor. Asking them stuff was a waste of time.

"Tell Ollie," I said, "that if he keeps annoying me, I will stop by and tie a knot in his pecker."

Long Hair nodded.

"Beat it," I said.

Long Hair and Baldy got slowly to their feet. They got Comb-over up, still bent over in pain, and got him into the backseat of the Crown Vic. Tedy Sapp bent over and picked up Comb-over's gun and looked at it and nodded to himself and slipped it into the pocket of his peacoat. The Crown Vic started up and pulled away. At Berkeley Street it turned right, heading for Storrow Drive, and we didn't see it anymore.

"You know the part about tying a knot in somebody's pecker," Sapp said.

"I was trying for a colorful metaphor," I said.

"Sure," Sapp said. "But if it happens, can I be the one does it?"

"God," I said. "I gotta find me some straight help."

Sapp grinned.

· 17 ·

April had an apartment on the fourth floor of the
mansion. We were up there eating oatmeal cookies and
drinking coffee. The apartment was nice in the unengag-
ing way that good hotel rooms are nice. There were
some paintings on the walls that went just right with the
room. There were no photographs of anyone anywhere
that I could see.

"Two of the girls quit today," April said. "Bev and another girl."

"Bev's the one that got beat up," I said.

April nodded.

"Are you making any progress?" she said. "I'm going
to lose more girls, I know I am. And the clients who were
here when those two apes rampaged through here . . ."

"Before Hawk and I joined the operation?" I said.

These oatmeal cookies had no raisins in them. I was pleased. I always thought raisins ruined oatmeal cookies.

"Yes," she said. "Those clients will never be back."

I nodded. April looked very nice today. Very pretty. Very pulled together. Very grown-up. She was wearing tan pants and a simple cobalt-colored top unbuttoned at the throat. They were expensive clothes and they fit her well.

"You need to do something," she said.

She was sitting on the couch, and when she spoke she put her cup down on the coffee table and leaned forward toward me.

"He's going to destroy me," she said.

"You mean he'll destroy your business."

"For me that's the same thing," April said. "This business is my life, the first time I've ever had something that was mine, that I could build and nurture."

"So why would he destroy that?" I said.

"What?"

"Why would he destroy your business. What would he get if he does?"

"Because he's crazy," she said. "Because he's cruel. Because he's a wretched pig of a man. I don't know. How do I know why he does what he does?"

"And you don't know who he is," I said.

"Of course not," April said.

Her face had flushed a little bit.

"If I knew who he was," she said, "why wouldn't I tell you so you could stop him?"

"And there's nothing you know that I don't know," I said.

"Oh my God, you don't believe me?"

"Just asking," I said.

She put her face in her hands and began to cry. I waited. I took the occasion while I was waiting to eat another raisin-free oatmeal cookie. She continued to cry. I went and sat on the couch beside her and put my arms around her.

"Nothing we can't fix," I said. "Whatever the truth is, it's nothing we can't fix."

She turned her face into my chest and cried some more. I patted her shoulder. The crying slowed. She wriggled against me a little and raised her head and looked at me. I smiled at her. Suddenly she leaned in against me and kissed me with her mouth open and tried to put her tongue in my mouth. I was horrified. It was like getting French-kissed by your daughter. I turned my head.

"April," I said.

She had squirmed herself on top of me as I leaned back against the corner of the couch, so that she pressed full-length against me.

"You've never touched me," she said. "Not since you met me. You've never touched me."

"You were pretty young," I said.

"And now I'm not," she said.

Her face was so close to mine that her lips brushed my face when she spoke.

"Too late," I said. "It would be like incest."

She was moving her body against me as she lay on me.

"Wouldn't you like to fuck me?" she said. "I'm good-looking and I'm really good at it."

"No," I said.

"Just once? Fuck me just once? I really know how."

I sat somewhat forcibly up and got my arms under her and stood up with her, and turned and set her back on the couch. She was still, flopped back as if she were exhausted, looking at me with her eyes half closed.

"You know you want to," she said. "Men always want to."

I looked at her for a moment without speaking.

Then I said, "Thanks for the offer," and turned and left the apartment.

·18·

Susan was back from Albany. She smiled when I finished my recitation.

"I guess April didn't want to talk about the case," Susan said.

"You think?"

Susan nodded.

"I do," she said. "And I have a Ph.D. from Harvard."

We had ordered dinner in Excelsior, at a table by the window, looking out over the Public Garden, and we were having cocktails while we waited.

"It's all she knows how to do," I said.

"And quite well," Susan said, "if you were reporting accurately."

"She says she does it quite well," I said.

"It's not terribly difficult to do well," Susan said.

"May I say you've mastered it," I said.

"Must I remind you again of the Harvard Ph.D.?" she said.

"Wow," I said, "they got courses in everything."

Susan took a small sip of her Cosmopolitan.

"It's a refrain I hear often," Susan said. "From patients. Women who are sexually active and have a limited skill set often brag about how good they are at sex."

"It's not really a matter of technique," I said.

"Fortunately for you," Susan said.

"Hey," I said.

She smiled.

"It has much to do," Susan said, "with whether you are happy in the task."

"So maybe she protesteth too much?"

"I'm sure she knows all there is to know," Susan said. "But most adult women do."

"Not all of them."

"There are a thousand things that can inhibit someone's sexuality. But lack of skill is not a common problem."

"Really," I said. "You didn't learn any of this up in Albany, did you?"

She grinned at me. The big, wide grin, full of things hinted but not exactly said.

"I haven't cheated on you in ages," Susan said.

"Good to know," I said.

"But, I was a grown woman when I met you," Susan said. "Remember? Married and divorced. I had already learned a lot of things."

I nodded.

"And there was that little business out west," she said.

"That was then," I said. "This is now."

She looked steadily at me with no banter. My hand was on the table. She put her hand on top of it.

"Yes," she said. "It is."

We were silent. I drank some scotch. She drank some Cosmopolitan.

"I'm running around this thing like a headless chicken," I said.

"My guess would be," Susan said, "that whatever answers you're likely to get will come out of April."

"She denies all," I said.

"She has a past," Susan said. "Maybe that will tell you something."

I nodded slowly, thinking about it.

"What got her in trouble last time?" Susan said.

"Looking for love in all the wrong places."

"And the time before that," Susan said. "When you first met her?"

"Looking for love in all the wrong places," I said.

"Without some sort of major intervention," Susan said, "people don't change much."

"Cherchez l'homme," I said.

Susan nodded. "Maybe," she said.

"You Ivy Leaguers are a smart lot, aren't you?"

Susan nodded vigorously.

"Wildly oversexed, too," she said.

"Not all of you," I said.

"One's enough," she said.

"Yes," I said. "It is."

I raised my glass toward her. She picked up hers. We clinked.

"Fight fiercely, Harvard," I said.

·19·

In New York I stayed at the Carlyle hotel. I could have stayed at a Days Inn on the West Side for considerably less. But I would have gotten considerably less, and I'd had a good year. I liked the Carlyle.

Thus, on a bright, windy day in New York, with the temperature not bad in the upper thirties, I sat with Patricia Utley in the Gallery on the Madison Avenue side of the hotel and had tea. It was elegant with velvet and dark wood. Faintly from the café I could hear piano music, somebody rehearsing for the evening. Barbara Carroll? Betty Buckley? I felt like I was in Gershwin's New York. I was more sophisticated than Paris Hilton.

"A professional thug," I said. "And a whorehouse madam having tea at the Carlyle. Is this a great country or what?"

"We look good," Patricia Utley said. "It covers a multitude."

We did look good. I looked like I always do: insouciant, roguish, and quite similar to Cary Grant, if Cary had had his nose broken more often. Patricia Utley wore a blue pin-striped pantsuit and a white shirt with a long collar. Her short hair had blond highlights, just like April's. Her makeup was discreet. She looked in shape. And the hints of aging at the corners of her face seemed to add some sort of prestige to her appearance.

We ordered the full tea. I like everything about tea, except tea. But I tried to stay with the spirit of it all.

"I've been chasing my tail," I said, "since I started with April."

Patricia Utley sipped some tea and put her cup down.

"And you wish my help?" she said.

"I do."

We both paused to examine our tea sandwich options.

"Let me tell you what I know, and what I think," I said.

"Please."

She listened quietly, sipping her tea, nibbling a cucumber sandwich. She seemed interested. She didn't interrupt.

When I was finished, she said, "You think there's a lover or ex-lover somewhere in the picture?"

"I think I should find out if there is."

"What do you need from me?" she said.

"Information."

"Information is problematic," Patricia Utley said. "I am in a business that deeply values discretion."

"Me too," I said.

She smiled.

"So we will be discreet with one another," she said.

"I need to have some names, someplace to start," I said. "Can you give me a list of her clients in the last year, say, when she was with you in New York?"

"Why would you think that I would have such a list."

"You're a woman of the twenty-first century," I said. "You have a database of clients in your computer, or my name is not George Clooney."

"You're bigger than George Clooney," Patricia Utley said.

"Yeah, but otherwise . . ." I said.

"An easy mistake to make," she said.

"I won't compromise you," I said. "But I need to see if she had a more than, ah, professional encounter with any of them."

She had some more tea, and a scone, while she thought about it.

"I have learned not to trust anyone," she said.

I waited.

"But oddly," she said, "I trust you."

I smiled my self-effacing smile, the one where I cock my head to the side a little.

"Good choice," I said.

"You won't compromise me," she said.

"Of course I won't."

"Of course you won't."

"So I get the list?" I said.

"I'll have it delivered to you tomorrow," she said. "Here."

"Oh good," I said. "I'll pay for tea."

·20·

The list of April's regular partners was a good one. There were about fifteen names on it; each was annotated with the dates of contact, how they paid, how to reach them, what their preferences were. I was pleased to see that their preferences were within normal parameters.

The direct approach might not be productive: *Hi, I'm a private detective from Boston. I'd like to talk with you about your long-term relationship with a professional prostitute.* I decided to consult a New York professional. And I knew who to call.

I met Detective Second Grade Eugene Corsetti for lunch at a Viand coffee shop on Madison Avenue, a couple of blocks uptown from the hotel. We sat in a tight booth on the left wall. It was tight for me, and Corsetti was as big as I was but more latitudinal. He was built like a bowling ball. But not as soft. I ordered coffee and a tongue sandwich on light rye. Corsetti had corned beef.

"How can you eat tongue," Corsetti said.

"You know how intrepid I am."

"Oh, yeah, I forgot that for a minute."

"You make first yet?" I said.

"Detective First Grade?" Corsetti said. "You got a better chance of making it than I have."

"And I'm not even a cop anymore," I said.

"Exactly," Corsetti said.

The coffee came. Corsetti put about six spoonfuls of sugar in his and stirred noisily.

"Is that because you annoy a lot of people?" I said.

"Yeah, sure," Corsetti said. "Always have. It's a gift."

The sandwiches came, each with half a sour pickle and a side of coleslaw. Corsetti stared at my sandwich.

"You're gonna eat that?" he said.

I nodded happily.

"Want a bite?" I said.

"Uck!" Corsetti said.

"You remember first time I met you?" I said.

Corsetti had a mouthful of sandwich. He nodded as he chewed.

"You were looking for a missing hooker," he said after he had swallowed and patted his mouth with his napkin.

"April Kyle," I said.

"Yeah," Corsetti said. "And somebody involved in it got killed a few blocks east of here, I think."

I nodded.

"And I caught the squeal," Corsetti said. "And there you were."

"And a few years later, at Rockefeller Center?"

"Heaven," Corsetti said. "I got a lot of face time on the tube out of that one. Whatever happened to the guy you had hold of."

"We arranged something," I said.

"Lot of that going around," Corsetti said. "Whaddya want now?"

"Renew acquaintances?" I said.

"Yeah, sure, want to hold hands and sing 'Kum By fucking Ya'?"

"I'm working on April Kyle again," I said.

"The same whore? She run off again?"

"No," I said. "She's in trouble."

"And her a lovely prostitute," Corsetti said. "How could that be?"

"I have a list of names; I was wondering if you could run them. See if any of them are in the system anyplace."

"Where'd you get the list?"

"They're former clients of April Kyle."

"So they'll be thrilled to have their names run," Corsetti said.

"We hope they won't know," I said.

"Who's we?"

"Me and the madam who gave me the list," I said.

"I ain't vice," Corsetti said. "I don't give a fuck about whores. What are you looking for?"

Corsetti was through eating. All I had left on my plate was half a pickle. I ate it.

"There's some sort of cherry pie over there on the counter," I said. "Under the glass dome."

"Yeah," Corsetti said. "I spotted it when I come in."

"I'm not going to have any," I said.

"No, me either," Corsetti said. "You gonna tell me what you're doing?"

"Okay," I said, and told him.

As I was telling him the waiter cleared our plates. I paused.

"Anything else?" the waiter said.

"More coffee," Corsetti said. "And two pieces of the cherry pie. Some cheese."

"You got it," the waiter said and walked away.

Corsetti and I poisoned ourselves with pie and cheese, while I finished explaining. When I was done, Corsetti put out his hand.

"Gimme the list," he said. "I'll get back to you."

· 21 ·

I spun my wheels for a couple of days until I finally met Corsetti again, this time in Grand Central Station.

"Why here?" I said as we sat together on a bench in the vast vaulted waiting room. Each of us had coffee in a plastic cup.

"I like it here," Corsetti said. "I come here when I get a chance."

The light was streaming in from the high windows. The room was busy with people. It was New York from another time, lingering into the twenty-first century. Corsetti handed me a big manila envelope.

"Here's your list back," Corsetti said. "I made some notes. You can go over it later."

"Anything good?" I said.

"I only got one guy," Corsetti said. "Lionel Farnsworth."

"What'd he do?" I said.

"LF Real Estate Consortium," Corsetti said. "Bought a bunch of slab two-bedroom ranches in North Jersey. Foreclosure junk. And resold them for a lot more to yuppies in Manhattan with the promise of high rental income and positive cash flow. He took a packaging fee on the deal and arranged the financing, for which he got a finder's fee from the bank."

"And?"

"Some of the property was condemned. Most of the houses needed rehab. Residents couldn't pay the rent. And the yuppies were left holding a bagful of garbage."

"And one of them got a lawyer," I said.

"They got together and got one," Corsetti said. "And he went to the Manhattan DA. And Manhattan talked to our cousins in Jersey."

"And?"

"Because the crime was interstate, Jersey and New York, the Feds got involved. There were some really swell turf battles, but eventually Lionel did two years in Allenwood, for some sort of interstate conspiracy to defraud."

"White Deer, Pennsylvania," I said.

"Sounds like a vacation spot," Corsetti said.

"Minimum security pretty much is," I said. "Got dates?"

"It's all in there," Corsetti said. "I'm just giving you highlights."

"Nobody else in the system?" I said.

"Nope."

A bum came shambling past us.

"You gen'lemen got some change?" he said.

Corsetti reached for his wallet. When he did, his coat fell open and the bum could see the gun and the shield clipped onto Corsetti's belt next to it. The bum backed away.

"Never mind," he said. "I didn' mean nothing."

Corsetti took out his wallet.

"Step over here," Corsetti said.

"Yessir."

The bum shuffled back. He didn't look at either of us. He looked at the floor. His shoulders hunched a little as if maybe Corsetti was going to hit him.

"I got no change," Corsetti said.

He handed the bum a ten-dollar bill. The bum took it and stared at it. He still didn't look at Corsetti, or me.

"Beat it," Corsetti said.

"Yessir," the bum said. "God bless."

He backed away with the bill in his hand, still looking at it, then turned and walked away across the waiting room under the high arched roof toward 42nd Street.

"Fucking stumblebums," Corsetti said. "The uniform guys come through couple times a day, sweep 'em out, but they're right back in here a half-hour later."

"Especially in the winter," I said. "Is 'stumblebum' the acceptable term for our indigent brothers and sisters?"

"Sometimes I like 'vagrants,'" Corsetti said. "Depends on how much style they got."

"Think the money will help him?" I said.

Robert B. Parker

"Nope."

"Think he'll spend it on booze?"

"Yep."

"So why'd you give it to him?" I said.

Corsetti swallowed the last of his coffee and grinned at me.

"Felt like it," he said.

· 22 ·

I spent an hour looking at Patricia Utley's list as annotated by Eugene Corsetti. Corsetti had thoughtfully located all fifteen guys by address and phone number for me. And he had included copies of Farnsworth's mug shots from when they'd made the first fraud arrest in 1998. Other than that, Corsetti didn't add much to what he had told me in the waiting room. I wanted to take a look at Lionel Farnsworth, so I walked across the park to where he lived, about opposite the Carlyle, in one of those impressive buildings that front Central Park West.

I wasn't sure what I thought I'd learn. The mug shots were old enough so that he might have changed, certainly. And people don't always look just like themselves when they're being booked. He would look different in the flesh. And I had some half-articulated sense that if he looked wrong for the part, I'd know it. Besides, I couldn't think of anything else to do.

There was a doorman at the entrance. He was a bulky guy wearing a maroon uniform with some braid. He had one of those New York Irish faces that implied he'd be perfectly happy to knock you down and kick you if you gave him any trouble.

"Lionel Farnsworth," I said.

The doorman took the phone from its brass box on the wall.

"Who shall I say?"

"Clint Hartung," I said.

"Spell the last name?"

"H-A-R-T-U-N-G," I said. "Hartung."

The doorman turned away and called. He spoke into the phone for a minute and turned back to me.

"Mr. Farnsworth doesn't recognize the name," he said. "He'd like to know what it's in regard to."

"Tell him it's in regard to matters we discussed in White Deer, Pennsylvania, a while back, when we were both visiting there."

The doorman relayed that into the phone and then listened silently for a moment, nodding. Then he hung up the phone and closed the little brass door.

"Mr. Farnsworth says he'll be down. You can wait in the lobby."

I went in. It was a small lobby done in black marble and polished brass. There was a bench on either side of the elevator door. They were upholstered in black leather. I sat on one. In maybe two minutes I heard the elevator coming down. And in another minute the doors opened and there he came. I stood.

"Mr. Farnsworth?" I said.

He turned toward me and smiled. He had his hand in his coat pocket, with the thumb showing. The thumbnail gleamed.

"Yes," he said. "What's this about White Deer?"

He was a really good-looking guy. About my height but slimmer. His dark hair had just enough gray highlights. It was longish and wavy and brushed straight back. He had a nice tan, and even features, and very fine teeth. He was wearing light gray slacks and a dark double-breasted blazer, and, God help us, a white silk scarf.

"I knew you were down there at Allenwood for a couple of years," I said. "Just a ploy to get you to see me."

Farnsworth's smile remained warm and welcoming. He glanced casually through the glass front door where the doorman was watching us. Then he took his hand from his coat pocket and stuck it out.

"Well, it worked, didn't it," he said. "And so delicately done. White Deer, Pennsylvania."

We shook hands, he gestured gracefully toward the bench where I'd been sitting, and both of us sat down on it. He shifted slightly so he could look me square in the eye.

"So," he said. "What can I help you with?"

Pretty good. No attempt to explain why he'd been at Allenwood. No outrage at being tricked. Just frank and friendly. No wonder people gave him their money. Frank and Friendly Farnsworth. Ready to deal with what is. And of course the doorman was handy, if things didn't go well.

"I've been employed by a big law firm, Gordon, Kerr, Rigney and Mize," I said. "They brought and won a class-action suit against a big national corporation, the name of which I'm not at liberty to divulge."

"Well, by God, good for them," Farnsworth said.

"Yeah," I said. "For once the good guys won. The settlement is, well, just let me tell you it is substantial, and a number of individuals are entitled to a considerable piece of change. If we can find them."

"You're not going to tell me I'm one of them?" Farnsworth said.

"Wish I could," I said. "But no, I'm looking for someone named April Kyle, and I have reason to believe you might know her."

"April," he said. "April, what was the last name?"

"Kyle," I said. "Like Kyle Rote."

"Kyle Rote?"

"Never mind," I said. "Do you know where I could find her?"

"April Kyle," he said. "I don't really think I know anybody named April Kyle."

Okay, so Lionel lies.

"Are you married, Mr. Farnsworth?"

"No," he said. "Not at the moment."

He smiled a big, open, engaging smile at me.

"Between gigs," he said. "Sort of."

I knew people often didn't brag about hiring prostitutes, but if he were single, he had less reason to lie, and there was serious money kicking around in this deal, and he might get some of it if he helped April to get hers. I almost smiled. My story was so good I was starting to believe it. A guy like Farnsworth would have sniffed around this situation. He didn't. And that was odd.

"Between gigs can be good or bad," I said.

He gave me a warm between-us-guys smile.

"At the moment, it's pretty damn good," he said.

"Congratulations," I said.

After we had shared our male moment, I stood.

"Thanks for your help, Mr. Farnsworth."

"Sorry I wasn't more useful," he said. "How'd you happen to come across that Allenwood thing?"

"Routine investigation," I said. "It won't even be in my report."

"Good," he said. "I could explain it but it's a bother."

"Don't give it a second thought," I said.

He smiled and nodded. We shook hands. As I left, I brushed against his right side. There was a gun in his right-hand jacket pocket.

"Oh," I said. "I'm sorry."

"No harm," he said.

"God," I said, "I'm clumsy."

"No problem," he said.

I went out of the lobby and passed the doorman. He watched me closely. I crossed with the light. The doorman was still watching me, and continued to watch me until I crossed into the park.

In Farnsworth's defense, it hadn't felt like a very big gun.

· 23 ·

Frank Belson and I had breakfast at the counter of a joint on Southampton Street, not far from the new police headquarters.

"Nice call," Belson said. "Ollie DeMars done time, for assault at MCI Concord 1990 to '92, *and* in the federal pen at Allenwood in 1998. So he was there the same time as your guy."

"Lionel Farnsworth," I said. "What was the federal charge?"

"Him and another guy were stealing pension checks from mailboxes. Ollie rolled on the other guy and got off with a year, easy time."

"That's our Ollie," I said. "Stand-up guy."

"Standing up for Ollie," Belson said. "I called the prison. Both of them were in the minimum-security part.

Robert B. Parker

Guy I talked with said it would be surprising if they didn't know each other."

I had a bite of corned beef hash. Belson drank coffee.

"What do you know about Ollie?" I said.

"I don't know him myself," Belson said. "But I asked around. Talked to OC squad, couple detectives in his precinct."

"Ollie qualify for organized-crime attention?"

"Not really. He's not that organized. But a lot of the organized outfits use him. He's got a sort of loose confederation of street-soldier wannabes that he'll rent out for strongarm work."

"He needs to hire better help," I said.

"To deal with you? Hawk? Sure he does. But his people are fine for slapping around some no-credit guy from Millis, borrowed money to open a restaurant and is behind on the vig."

"Ollie do any of his own work?"

"Mostly he runs things. But he's tough enough to run them. He can keep the wannabes in line," Belson said.

I ate some more hash. Belson's breakfast was an English muffin and coffee. No wonder he was lean.

"He's not necessarily a loyal person," I said.

"Guy in the mailbox deal is probably still in Allenwood, doing Ollie's time," Belson said.

I finished my hash. Frank took a bite out of his English muffin. I looked at his plate. He was still on the first half of the muffin.

"Is that all you eat for breakfast?" I said.

"I drink a lot of coffee," Belson said.

"That's nourishing," I said.

"I'm never hungry much," Belson said. "I eat enough to stay alive."

"Me too," I said.

The counter man cleared my plate. I ordered more coffee and a piece of pineapple pie. Belson put some grape jelly on his remaining half a muffin.

"Fruit," Belson said.

"You healthy bastard," I said.

"Ollie ain't a major leaguer," Belson said. "Because he ain't the brightest bulb on the tree. But people who know say he's got a big ego, and he's pretty crazy, and most people don't take him on if they don't have to."

"I may have to," I said.

Belson nodded.

"Speaking of ego," Belson said.

"I like to think of it as self-confidence," I said.

"I'm sure you do," Belson said.

"He's annoyed Tony Marcus," I said. "It is an article of religious faith with Tony that whore business is black business."

"Tony believes that about any business he's in," Belson said.

"His faith is flexible," I said.

"Tony would win that one," Belson said. "Why don't you let him."

"Tony wants to give me a chance to neutralize Ollie. Probably doesn't want you guys on his ass."

"Yeah, and we'd be all over him, working night and day and day and night to find out who aced a creep like Ollie DeMars."

"I'm just reporting the news," I said. "I'm not making it."

"You gonna talk with him?"

"Ollie?" I said. "Yeah."

"Why don't I go along, flash the badge. That way you probably won't have to shoot anybody."

"Thanks for caring," I said. "How crazy is Ollie?"

"Not crazy enough to shoot a cop," Belson said.

· 24 ·

Belson was on the radio during the short drive to Andrews Square, and we parked outside Ollie's place for a few minutes.

"I may have to talk about stuff that might not be legal," I said. "I hope you won't overhear it."

"Huh?" Belson said.

I nodded.

"Okay," I said.

Some uniforms pulled up in a couple of cruisers. We got out. Belson went and talked to the uniforms, and came back to me. He took out his badge, clipped it onto the lapel of his topcoat, and he and I went into the storefront.

There were three people I didn't know out in the front. One of them, a husky guy with a blond ponytail, got up when he saw us and walked down the hall. In a moment he came back with Ollie beside him. Ollie looked at me as if he had never seen me before. He looked at the badge on Belson's lapel and smiled.

"Yessir, officer," Ollie said. "How can I help you?"

"Let's talk in your office," Belson said.

"Sure," Ollie said and walked back down the hall.

We followed. When he was behind his desk, he leaned back and put his feet up and spread his hands.

"Do I need a lawyer here?" he said.

"Naw," Belson said. "We're all friends here. You know Spenser?"

Ollie's eyes widened and he looked at me carefully.

"Oh," Ollie said. "Sure. I didn't recognize you. How ya doing?"

Ollie was wearing a tattersall shirt today, and a black knit tie, and a sand-colored corduroy jacket.

"Swell," I said. "Tell me about your friendship with Lionel Farnsworth."

Ollie stared at me unblinking for a minute, then looked at Belson.

"He's no cop," Ollie said.

"Tell me about your friendship with Lionel Farnsworth," Belson said.

Ollie looked at Belson and back at me.

"Who?" he said to Belson.

Belson grinned without warmth.

"It can go quick," Belson said, "you talk with Spenser. It'll take a lot longer he asks, you look at me, I ask again."

Ollie shrugged. The suburban Rotarian veneer was getting thin.

"I guess so," he said.

"So," I said, "tell me about your friendship with Lionel Farnsworth."

"I don't know him," Ollie said.

"You do," I said. "You were in Allenwood federal prison with him in 1998."

"I was there, yeah, on a bad rap, by the way, but I didn't know anybody named Farnswhatever."

"And when he needed some arm-twisting done for him up here," I said, "seven years later, he called you."

"I ain't doing no strong-arm work for Farnsworth."

Belson was tilted back slightly in his chair, one foot cocked on the edge of Ollie's desk.

"Ollie," he said. "You are making a liar out of me. I said you didn't need a lawyer, and now you are shoveling so much shit at us that, maybe you keep doing it, you are going to need one."

"For what?" Ollie said.

Without the glad-handed good-guy disguise, Ollie's natural stupidity began to dominate. He even sounded different. *Bullshit is only skin deep.*

"Just listen to me for a minute," I said. "You sent some guys over to the mansion, and Hawk and I kicked their ass. Then you sent four guys to chase me off the case, and Tedy Sapp and I kicked their ass. Now I know who hired you to do it, and when I confront him with these facts, he'll claim it was all your doing and he just wanted you to talk with April."

"At which time," Belson said, "we in the Boston Police Department will feel obligated to protect and serve your ass right into the fucking hoosegow."

"Or," I said, "you can flip on old Lionel now, while the flipping is good, and tell us your side of the story before we even talk with Lionel."

"What about the assault stuff," Ollie said.

"I don't need to press charges on those," I said. "Hell, I won both fights anyway."

"Okay," he said.

He stood suddenly and walked to his office door and closed it.

"Okay," he said again.

He walked back to his desk and sat down. The jolliness was back. He wasn't confused now. He knew what to do.

"I'll tell you about Farnsworth," he said.

· 25 ·

My last serious talk with April had ended badly, so this time I talked with her in the front parlor of the mansion, with Hawk and Tedy Sapp present in case she attempted to seduce me again. She had been sulky since I'd rejected her, and she was sulky now.

"I've located Lionel Farnsworth," I said.

She had no reaction.

"You know him, don't you?" I said.

"No."

"He was with you twenty-three times in the year before you came up here," I said.

She shrugged.

"They're all johns," she said.

I nodded.

"I've had a talk with Ollie DeMars," I said.

"Who?"

"The gentleman who's been managing the harassment," I said. "He tells me that he was hired to do that by a gentleman he once knew in Allenwood prison, a man from New York named Lionel Farnsworth."

"I thought it was someone with an offshore bank account," April said.

"Ollie made that up," I said. "It was his old prison pal Lionel."

April didn't say anything.

"What we have here," I said, "is a remarkable coincidence. The guy who is extorting you is a guy you have known professionally at least twenty-three times."

She shrugged again.

"I have prevailed upon Ollie to leave you alone," I said.

"You think he will?" April said.

"Yes."

"Then I don't need you anymore," April said.

"That depends on how earnest Lionel is," I said.

"I told you I don't know Lionel."

"April," I said. "What the hell is going on?"

"Nothing," April said. "This Ollie person has been stopped. Thank you. That's all I need."

Hawk stood up.

"Our work here is done," he said to Tedy Sapp.

Sapp grinned.

"Ollie was no match for us," Sapp said.

He turned to April.

"I'll pack and be gone in an hour," he said. "Nice doing business with you."

"Say good-bye to the ladies," Hawk said.

April nodded. She didn't say anything. Hawk and Sapp left. April and I sat. The silence continued. *She cannot have lived the life she's led,* Susan had said, *without suffering a lot of damage. Under stress,* she had said, *the damage usually surfaces.*

"There's nothing so bad I can't hear it," I said.

She nodded.

"There's nothing so bad I won't help you with it," I said.

She kept nodding. I stood.

"Okay, Toots," I said. "No lectures. If you find that you need me again, you know where I am."

"Yes," she said.

I went to where she sat and bent over and kissed her. She stiffened slightly. I stepped back and pretended to shoot her with my forefinger, and turned and left.

· 26 ·

Hawk drove Tedy Sapp to the airport. I went, too.
Now that I was off the case, I had nothing else to do.
And it gave me a chance to see if the tunnel was leaking
today.

"April didn't like you," Hawk said to Tedy Sapp.

"No," Sapp said. "She didn't."

"I'm not sure she liked any of us."

"Worse with Tedy," Hawk said. "He being gay
and all."

"Lot of women like gay men," Sapp said. "They can
talk about things comfortably. . . ."

"Like pottery," Hawk said. "Hair tint."

Sapp ignored him.

"Without any sexual tension, so to speak. And, as we
all know, gay men are urbane, witty, sophisticated, and
unusually charming."

"Some of Ollie's people," I said, "can testify to that."

"But . . ." Hawk said.

Sapp nodded.

"But there are some women who are uncomfortable with us precisely because there's no sexual tension," Sapp said. "They can't use sex to control us. Flirting with us isn't effective."

"That's true of a lot of straight men, too," I said.

"Sure," Sapp said. "Probably true of you."

"Might want to ask Susan 'bout that," Hawk said.

"That's love," I said.

"Um," Hawk said.

"But even though that's true," Sapp said, "a woman like April can create a sexual tone to her male relationships that she can't do with a ho-mo-sex-u-al."

"Sex is the only thing that ever worked for her," I said.

"And that sure worked out good," Hawk said.

"She knows that guy in New York," Sapp said. "Doesn't she."

I nodded.

"You gonna let it slide?" Sapp said.

Hawk laughed.

"You done a couple riffs with him," Hawk said. "What you think he gonna do?"

"I think he's going to chew on this," Sapp said, "like a beaver on a tree."

"You going to New York?" Hawk said.

"I am," I said.

"Gonna talk with Farnsworth?" he said.

"Seems like a good idea," I said.

"Then what?" Hawk said.

"Depends on what he says."

"How 'bout he says for you to go fuck yourself," Sapp said.

"Why should he be different?" I said.

"Spenser don't like Farnsworth the way he like April," Hawk said.

"So you might be more forceful," Sapp said.

"We have our ways," I said.

"Anybody paying you?" Sapp said.

"I'm getting twice what you're getting," I said.

"I'm getting zip," Sapp said.

"And worth every penny," I said.

Hawk pulled into the curb in front of the Delta terminal.

"Least Robin Hood stole it," he said, "'fore he gave it away."

"And," Sapp said, "he had all those merry men."

·27·

I used a different technique with Lionel Farnsworth this time. The lawyer-with-money trick probably wouldn't play twice, with either him or the doorman. So I began to hang out near his building on a bright, crisp New York day. In the late afternoon of the first day, he came out of his building wearing a belted double-breasted camel-hair overcoat and turned right on Central Park West, toward Columbus Circle. I fell in beside him.

"Nothing like a brisk stroll," I said. "Huh?"

He looked at me and did a little repressed double take.

"You," he said.

"Me."

"Ah . . . the, ah, lawyer guy, right?"

"Sort of," I said.

"Sort of?"

"I lied to you."

He stopped.

"You lied?"

"I did," I said. "I'm a detective."

"A detective."

"Exactly," I said.

We began to walk again.

"New York City police?" he said.

"I'm from Boston," I said.

He looked at me and started to speak and decided not to. His pace had picked up a little. I stayed with him.

"Ollie DeMars spilled the beans," I said.

"Ollie DeMars?"

"Yep."

"I don't believe I know him."

"You do," I said. "You were in Allenwood with him. Six months ago you called him and hired him to harass April Kyle. You told him don't kill anybody. And don't hurt April but keep on her case until you say to stop."

"He's lying," Farnsworth said. "Who's April Kyle?"

"I don't think he's lying," I said.

"He is," Farnsworth said. "Are you going to believe some ex-con felon like him?"

"As opposed to an ex-con felon like you?"

"That was a mistake," Farnsworth said. "I was innocent of any wrongdoing."

"And they sent you to Allenwood why?"

"Prosecutor wanted to make a name for himself."

"By putting a high-profile guy like you away," I said.

"Absolutely," Farnsworth said.

"So you know Ollie," I said, "after all."

"I remember him now," Farnsworth said. "From Allenwood. We barely knew each other. I don't know why he's saying these things about me."

"Jealousy probably," I said. "I have evidence, by the way, that you availed yourself of April's expertise at least twenty times in the year before she moved to Boston, and that you always requested her by name."

"He told you that?"

"No. I learned that elsewhere."

"Well I told you before, and I'm telling you now, I don't know any April Kyle."

"Lionel," I said. "I got witnesses who will testify that you were often in April Kyle's company and referred to her by name. I have the stalwart Ollie DeMars who will testify that you hired him to roust April Kyle, and referred to her specifically by name when you did so. Ollie says you wired him the money every week. It's only a matter of time before we find your bank and get a record of the transfer."

Farnsworth stared straight ahead as he walked. I walked with him and didn't say anything for a while. We got to Columbus Circle and stopped for the light.

"I'm not necessarily after you," I said.

Farnsworth stared up at the light.

"I can grind you on it, or I can let it kind of slide; depends pretty much on how much you're willing to talk with me. And what I hear."

The light changed. We started across.

"We'll go in the Time Warner Center," Farnsworth said, "and talk."

"Perfect," I said.

·28·

We sat on a leather sofa in front of a big window in the lobby area on the top floor of the Time Warner Center and looked out at Columbus Circle and the park beyond.

"Okay," Lionel said. "You got me. Yes, I patronized April Kyle regularly, when she was a working girl. Tell me you don't do that."

"I don't do that," I said.

"You married?"

"Sort of," I said.

He frowned at the *sort of* but didn't comment.

"Well," Lionel said, "I started out just because she was, you know, good."

I nodded.

"But"—he shook his head in an open, man-to-man way—"it's like some Broadway musical, you know? I fell for her."

I nodded.

"I'm still crazy about her," he said.

"How's she feel?" I said.

"Same way," he said. "We're crazy about each other."

"Which is why you hired Ollie DeMars," I said, "to put her out of business."

Farnsworth shook his head slowly.

"No, no," he said. "You don't get it. We're in business together. That place is just the first in a chain of what I like to call boutique whorehouses we were planning to start."

"Oh," I said. "*That's* why you hired Ollie DeMars to put her out of business."

Lionel shook his head again and looked at me as if I were a small boy.

"You'd never make it in the fast-shuffle business," he said. "You think too straight ahead."

"If at all," I said.

"We were scamming the madam, Utley. We pulled this scheme together to give her a reason to let go of the business and not require her money back. You unnerstand? Then we'd take it over, and that's all she wrote."

"So this is all just a con so that you and April can steal the business from Mrs. Utley."

"Steal's a little harsh. We'll develop it," he said, "beyond what she could imagine."

"And the mansion in Boston is your pilot program," I said.

"You bet," he said. "You like the mansion concept. My idea. We're going to call it Dreamgirl. The Dreamgirl mansions? You dig? And we'll have a tagline. *Love like a playboy*. You like it? *Love like a playboy at the Dreamgirl mansion in* . . . and you fill in the city. Huh? When it's up and really rolling, we can franchise the concept and sit back and collect the franchise fees."

"What if they don't pay the fee?" I said. "Not everybody who wants to franchise a whorehouse is a fully responsible citizen."

"We'd provide for that. I was going to use Ollie, but I guess I'll have to find someone else. That's not hard. There are always Ollies."

"So this being the case, and you and April being closer than clams in a cozy chowder," I said, "how come she hired me to make it all go away."

"Smoke screen," Farnsworth said.

"Not such a good one," I said.

"I know, we tried to get too cute. April said she could control you, and . . ." He shrugged. "I figured you were just another retired cop fleshing out his pension."

"And how do we feel about the hooker that got beat up on her way home from the movies one night."

"I heard about that. April was furious. Like I told her, my instructions to Ollie was that nobody get hurt. Ollie went too far, and I spoke to him about it and warned him against doing that again."

"Probably terrified him," I said.

Farnsworth shrugged.

"I was his employer," he said. "He followed my instructions or we got somebody else to do the work."

"A hard man is good to find," I said.

"Hey," Farnsworth said. "That's pretty clever. You make that up?"

"No."

He thought about it for a minute, and then laughed and patted his hand on the leather couch seat a couple of times.

"I'll bet some hot broad made it up," he said.

"Sure," I said. "That's probably what happened."

"A hard man is good to find," Farnsworth said. "That's great."

"Do you have a financial position in this enterprise?" I said.

"Sure, me and April are partners, everything's fifty-fifty."

"So how much you invested so far?" I said.

"Haven't needed to so far. We're sort of dining on Utley for the time. But I got some investors lined up, and when we start expanding, I'll be bringing in a lot of money. Want to jump in?" he said. "Chance to get in on the ground floor."

I shook my head.

"We're gonna be rich," he said. "Don't say I didn't give you your shot."

"Okay," I said.

"Maybe it should be *Live like a playboy*," Farnsworth said. "Or *Live and love like a playboy*."

"Or," I said, "how about, *I'll spend my life in litigation over trademark infringement.*"

"What copyright?" he said.

I shrugged.

"Just kidding around," I said.

We were quiet then, looking out the window past Columbus Circle, where there was still construction going on. And down 59th Street, where for several blocks it was called Central Park South. I didn't believe everything he was saying. But I wouldn't have believed everything he said if he told me the time. There was enough there that might be true for me to take back to April. I stood.

"Have a swell day," I said and turned and left him.

For the moment, at least, I'd had enough of the egregious bastard.

· 29 ·

The first thing April did was cry. We were sitting in her front parlor when I told her what Lionel Farnsworth had told me. I was halfway through when she began to cry. It was controlled at first, as if it were a ploy. But then it got away from her, and by the time I was through with Lionel's story, she was into a sobbing, shaking, nose-running, chest-heaving, gasping-for-breath, flat-out-crying fit.

"I gather I've touched a nerve," I said.

She sobbed. Her eyes were swollen. Her makeup was eroding. Except for the paroxysms of her crying, she was inert in her chair.

"Is Lionel telling me the truth?" I said.

She kept crying. She was hugging herself. Each sob made her body shudder as if it hurt. I waited. She cried. I was pretty sure I could wait longer than she could cry.

I was right.

After a time the crying slowed to heavy breathing. She sat silently for a time, then stood suddenly and walked out of the room. I waited some more. Dust motes danced in the oblique morning light. After maybe fifteen minutes, April came back into the room. She had probably washed her face in cold water and put on new makeup. Her eyes looked better.

She sat back down in the same chair and folded her hands in her lap and looked at me.

"In my whole life," she said softly, "I have never met a man that didn't betray me."

I wanted to claim an exclusion. But she seemed to be musing. And I thought it wise to let her muse.

"My father," she said. "Mr. Poitras. Rambeaux. Now it's Farnsworth."

I nodded.

"I guess I am not good at picking men."

"Maybe it's not a skill," I said.

"What do you mean."

"Maybe you do what you need to do."

"Oh, God," she said. "Just what I need right now, an amateur shrink."

"I know a professional one," I said.

"Fuck you," April said.

"Oh," I said. "Good point."

"I don't need some whacked-out therapist to tell me my life has sucked."

This wasn't an argument I was going to win today. I let it slide.

"So how much of Lionel's story should I believe?" I said.

She shrugged and didn't answer.

"Can I take that to mean all of it."

"No."

"How much?" I said.

"I don't want to talk about it," she said.

I nodded. We were quiet.

After a while I said, "Is there anything you want me to do before I leave?"

"Leave?"

"Yeah."

"You mean for good?"

"For a while," I said.

"You too," she said.

"Me too what?"

"You bastard." She started to cry again. "You fucking bastard."

"April," I said.

"Bastard, bastard, bastard."

I went back to the waiting game. She cried a little more, but not like before. This time she didn't have to leave the room. She stopped in maybe five minutes. Her eyes were red again. But her makeup was still okay. She sat in her chair and looked at nothing.

"So how much of Lionel's story should I believe?" I said.

She was hunched forward now, looking at the floor, with her clenched hands between her knees.

"We had a relationship," she said. "We met when he bought a night with me, and we liked each other, and he kept requesting me. Mrs. Utley was good that way. And after a while I started to see him on my own and not charge him. That was against the rules, but Mrs. Utley never knew. I saw him on my own time."

Her voice as she spoke was soft and flat. She seemed to be reciting a story she'd learned by rote about someone else.

"When Mrs. Utley sent me up here, he would come up to see me and spend the night. We talked about things. We'd lie in bed at night after and talk about going out on our own. We'd need a nest egg, he said, and he showed me how to skim some money on Mrs. Utley each day and she wouldn't know."

"So you could open a place of your own."

"Start a chain," she said.

"How long did you figure it would take you to embezzle enough to do that?"

"Not long. It was only for the down payment. Earnest money, he said. He said he was lining up investors."

"So what went wrong," I said.

She stared silently down.

"He cheated on me," she said.

"Anyone you know?"

"Yes. Here. One of the girls. In this house."

I nodded.

"He didn't pay her," April said.

"You sleep with an occasional customer," I said.

"He knows that and he knows it's business. It's not about us."

There was nothing for me down that road.

"So you broke up?" I said.

She nodded.

"How'd he take it."

"He acted like nothing had happened," she said.

"Denied everything?"

"Just pretended like I hadn't thrown him out or anything. Just said he knew I was upset."

"And left."

"Yes. He tried to kiss me good-bye," April said.

"You hear from him again?"

"A week later," April said. "He sent me a bill for what he called his share of the business."

"Ah, Lionel," I said.

"I sent it back to him," April said, "with *fuck you* written across it."

"And soon thereafter Ollie's people showed up," I said.

"Yes."

"And you came to me," I said, "hoping somehow I'd take them off your back without finding out what had happened."

"I was cheating Mrs. Utley. I had fallen for another loser and gotten in trouble. I didn't know what to do. I was too mortified to tell you the truth."

"And you thought I wouldn't find that out," I said.

"I don't know. I was alone, and scared, and ashamed, and you were the only person in my life who had ever actually helped me."

"Except Mrs. Utley," I said.

"I couldn't go to her. I was stealing from her."

I nodded.

"Hell," April said. "Maybe I wanted you to find out."

"Maybe," I said.

·30·

Susan had occasional small fits of domesticity. They passed quickly in most cases, but now and then one fell at the wrong time and she felt the need to make dinner for us. So there she was, wearing a nice-looking apron, standing at her kitchen counter preparing food.

"You believe April?" Susan said.

"More than I believe Lionel," I said.

"But not a lot more?" Susan said.

"I like her better," I said.

"It's good," Susan said, "that you don't let sentiment cloud your judgment."

"I'm a seasoned professional," I said.

"If she's telling the truth," Susan said, "then Lionel is, in effect, stalking her."

"Virtual stalking," I said. "He hired Ollie DeMars to do it."

"Doesn't matter. Stalking is about power and revenge and control, and who the physical stalker is doesn't matter if the real stalker gets the feelings he needs."

"Or she needs," I said.

"Of course. I was speaking of this particular incident. Women can be stalkers, too."

"How come you don't stalk me," I said.

"Don't need to," Susan said.

"Because you already have feelings of power and control?"

"Exactly," Susan said.

"Is that because I come across for you so easy," I said.

"It is."

"What if I didn't?" I said.

Susan smiled at me. She was halfway into the preparation for some sort of chicken in a pot. As she spoke she chopped carrots on a cutting board. It was slow going and I feared for her fingers, but I was smart enough to make no comment.

"Empty threat," she said. "What are you going to do about Lionel Whosie?"

"I could kill him," I said.

"No," Susan said, "you couldn't."

"No?"

"No. You would do that for me, maybe for Hawk. But not for April."

Susan began to peel onions. Her eyes were watering.

"If you peel those onions under running water," I said, "they won't make you tear up."

Susan nodded and continued to peel them without benefit of water. When she was done she quartered them and tossed them into the pot, after the carrots.

"How about the police?" Susan said.

"And April gets dragged into it," I said, "and probably Patricia Utley."

Susan smiled.

"They're whores," Susan said. "By choice. One could consider getting in trouble with the police an occupational risk."

I shook my head. Susan smiled.

"They may be whores," Susan said. "But they're your whores."

"Exactly," I said

Susan put some fresh parsley and some thyme into the pot, poured in some white wine, and put the cover on.

"This might actually be good," she said, "if I don't overcook it."

"How about setting the timer?" I said.

She looked at me scornfully, and took off her apron, and set the timer.

"So what shall we do while it cooks?" she said.

"We could drink and fool around," I said.

"Pearl's asleep on the bed," Susan said.

"I know," I said. "She likes that late-afternoon sun in there."

"But there is the couch," Susan said.

"There is," I said.

"First I think we should shower."

"Together?"

"Sure, get a clean start," Susan said.

"And if you put me under running water," I said, "you may not tear up."

Susan began to unbutton her shirt as she walked toward the bedroom.

"Oh," she said. "I probably will anyway."

·31·

I was drinking coffee and eating a corn muffin and reading the paper in my office with the window open and my feet on the desk. In mid-February the temperature was fifty-one, and the snow was melting as fast as it could. I had just finished reading Arlo & Janis when Quirk came in.

"Got a shooting," he said. "In Andrews Square. You might want to take a peek."

I took my paper, my coffee, and my muffin and went with him.

There were eight or ten cop cars, marked and unmarked, clogging nearly all movement in the area of Ollie DeMars's clubhouse. Belson walked to the car when it stopped. He looked in and saw me.

"Oh, good," Belson said. "You brought help."

We got out.

"Every citizen's duty," I said, "to step forward when needed."

"Try not to stomp on the clues," Quirk said as we went into the building.

There was no one from Ollie's crew in sight. Just Ollie, sitting in his chair behind his desk, with his head slumped forward and blood on his shirt. A couple of crime-scene types were photographing and writing notes and taking measurements.

"Whaddya got," Quirk said to one of them.

"Took one in the forehead, Captain. Small-caliber. Snapped his head back, and then forward."

The crime-scene guy demonstrated snapping his head back and letting it rebound forward.

"Probably dead before his head bounced," the crime-scene guy said. "And that's how we found him. No exit wound, so we'll be able to salvage the slug. Might be kind of beat up, rattling around inside a skull."

Quirk nodded.

"Muzzle was close to his forehead; there's burns."

Quirk nodded again.

"Gun in the desk drawer, loaded," the crime-scene guy said. "Not fired recently. Drawer was closed when we found him."

"Got an idea of when he died?" Quirk said.

"Not really," the crime-scene guy said. "Guess? Some-time last night. We'll know when they open him up."

"Lemme know," he said.

He looked at Belson.

"Who found the body?" Quirk said.

"Anonymous nine-one-one," Belson said. "From a pay phone in Watertown. First car here was Garvey and Nelson."

Belson nodded at a bulky uniformed cop standing near the office door.

"That's Garvey," Belson said.

"What?" Quirk said to him.

"Like you see it, Captain, nobody here but the stiff. He's right the way we found him. Me and Nelson secured the crime scene and called the detectives."

Quirk nodded. The room was full of cops, tough men who had spent most of their working hours on the hard side of life. But all of them were careful around Quirk. Except maybe Belson . . . and me.

"Any witnesses?" Quirk said.

Belson shook his head.

"So who did the nine-one-one?" Quirk said.

"Shooter?" Belson said.

"Why?" Quirk said.

"Can't imagine," Belson said.

Quirk looked at me.

"You got anything to say?"

"I've been here twice," I said. "There were always people sitting around the front room."

"So where were they when Ollie was getting clipped?"

Belson shook his head. Quirk looked at me. I shook my head.

"And why was Ollie's gun still in the drawer?" Quirk said.

"He knew the killer?" I said.

"Or the killer came in so fast and did him so quick he never got a chance at it," Belson said.

"Guy like Ollie doesn't usually sit around with no protection," Quirk said.

"Somebody wants to kill a guy like Ollie," I said, "doesn't normally walk into where he would be sitting around with protection."

"Maybe they knew he'd be alone," Belson said.

"Or that the protection wouldn't interfere," Quirk said.

"Somebody called it in," I said.

"One of Ollie's associates came in, saw him, didn't want to get involved," Belson said. "So he screws. But what if Ollie ain't dead? So he stops someplace and calls nine-one-one."

Quirk nodded without comment.

"Or somebody wants it known that he's dead," I said.

"Like a warning?" Quirk said

"Maybe," I said.

Quirk nodded again. He looked around the room. Then at Belson. Then at me.

"It is always a special treat," he said, "to find you involved in a nice homicide."

"Imagine my pleasure," I said.

Quirk didn't respond for a moment as he looked at the crime scene. Then he turned back to me.

"Frank's filled me in," Quirk said, nodding sideways at Belson, "a little on your involvement. But let's you and me sit in my car and go over it anyway."

"It is the duty of every citizen. . . ." I said.

"Yeah," Quirk said. "Yeah, yeah, yeah."

·32·

I sat in the front room of the mansion with April and her working girls. There were other people to talk with: the two women who worked in the office, the woman who tended bar, the woman who cooked, the woman who did the housekeeping. But April was adamant at keeping the two kinds of staff separate. So I talked with the professional staff first.

It was a good-looking group. Their makeup was understated. Their daytime wardrobe tended toward skirts and sweaters. Some of them were wearing penny loafers. I felt like it was 1957 and I was running a Tupperware party.

I explained how Ollie DeMars had been killed, and reminded them who Ollie was.

"The Homicide commander," I said, "cop named Martin Quirk, knows that a full-scale investigation will have to include you and could be a source of great embarrassment and serious hardship to all of you."

They all looked tense.

"He's willing to work around you for the moment. Let me do the investigating here."

They all looked a little less tense. Several of them were drinking coffee from mugs, holding the mugs in both hands.

"Don't be confused," I said. "This will not be a white-wash. If I uncover something germane, I will tell Quirk about it."

They tensed up a little more.

"Cops tell me he died around midnight on Monday night," I said. "Who's got an alibi?"

Everyone stared at me.

A cute blond woman with a blue headband said, "You think one of us might have killed somebody?"

"Just trying to eliminate anyone with an alibi," I said.

"So if I got one, does it mean I'm out of this."

"Means we don't think you did it," I said. "Doesn't mean you don't know anything."

"You wouldn't suspect us if we were a bunch of schoolteachers," the blonde said.

"What's your name?" I said.

"Darleen."

"I won't suspect you if you have an alibi, Darleen," I said. "Do you?"

She nodded.

"Tell me," I said.

"I can't," she said.

"Because?"

"I was with my husband. We went to a parents' meeting at the school, and my husband drove the babysitter home. Monday night midnight we were in bed together watching *Charlie Rose*."

"I see your problem," I said.

"We don't have any street sluts here," April said. "Most of my girls have a home life. It's one of the reasons I hired them."

"And if this life gets dragged into that life," I said, "itwill cause a lot of people a lot of pain they don't deserve."

April nodded.

"Unless they killed Ollie DeMars," I said.

"None of my girls killed anyone."

I nodded.

"And if they were with a client, the same kind of problem exists."

"We don't have confidentiality," April said, "we are out of business."

The women sat around the room watchfully.

I looked at them, one at a time.

"Anybody with an alibi they can tell me?" I said.

No one said anything.

"Hot dog!" I said.

Everyone was quiet.

"Okay," I said after a while. "We'll put that aside for the moment. We may visit it later, but right now let's just talk a little."

"About what?" another woman said. She had on a white shirt and a red plaid skirt and wore her dark hair in a Dorothy Hamill wedge.

"Everything, anything. What is your name?"

"Amy."

"Tell me about yourself. You married?"

"Yes."

"Kids."

"Yes."

"Where do you live?"

"Suburbs."

"And how'd you get into this business."

"You serious?" Amy said.

"Sure. I might as well get to know you."

I just wanted them talking. People liked nothing as much as talking about themselves. And Susan often reminded me that there was no way to know what might pop up in the course of talking about other things.

"You are serious," Amy said.

I nodded.

"You want to know how a married suburban mother ends up in a whorehouse."

I nodded.

She looked at the other women. They looked at her. She looked at April. April shrugged. She looked around at the other women again.

"Give him an earful," Darleen said. "He might learn something."

Two of the women giggled. Amy nodded.

"I tell him then you tell him?" she said to Darleen.

"You're on," she said.

·33·

Once the deluge began, it was nearly impossible to staunch. They were so thrilled to be talking about themselves that I thought I might have to shoot my way out of there.

Darleen wouldn't tell me where she lived, or what her last name was. She was married to a guy who worked nights. He was nice enough, a good father, but he was kind of boring. Not so boring she'd want to leave him, and she guessed she actually did love him. But she liked sex more than he did. She had fooled around almost since they married, and to her, the work at the mansion was just more fooling around, except she got paid. She had a nice mutual fund going for the kids, which her husband didn't know about, and she had a little mad money of her own, which her husband thought she earned with a pickup-and-delivery service in the suburban area where they lived. . . . Amy was a grad student, she wouldn't say where, and had been hooking up with guys since junior high. Like Darleen, she enjoyed sex, and when the tuition bills started piling in, she thought if she were going to do it anyway, maybe she should get paid. . . . Jan said that getting paid for sex made her feel empowered. All of them agreed that it did. They were items of value. . . . Kelly was divorced and supported two children and her mother. Mother looked after the kids while Kelly was working. . . . Emily was an airline attendant. . . . Kate was a third-grade teacher. . . . They all enjoyed sex. None of them felt exploited. . . . All of them enjoyed the free time that the work gave them. . . . They also, though they never quite knew how to say it, liked being a band of sisters. . . . Two of them had responded to April's solicitation on the Internet. Two more had been recruited by a charming man they met in a dating bar. No one would name him, but I assumed it was Lionel Farnsworth. . . .

"Everybody always talks about how prostitution exploits women," Amy said. "But I see it as exploiting men. They pay us for something we'd been doing for free. It's fun. And . . ." She giggled. "They'll do pretty much whatever you say when you have them excited."

The other women giggled with her.

"They are kind of pathetic," Kelly said.

"I had a guy always brought candy," Jan said. "I always threw it out after he left."

"A fat whore with zits, perfect," Emily said.

They all laughed.

"You know what else I like?" Darleen said. "I like working for April."

They all did a little hand clap.

"I mean, I don't want to sound like some women's lib crackpot," she said, "but it's nice to work for a woman in a woman's business."

They all clapped.

"I mean," Kate said, "there's no pimp. You know how nice that is?"

They clapped again.

"How about Lionel?" Amy said.

April frowned at her. But they were having too good a time talking about something they had probably never talked about—and to a man. No one responded to her frown.

"Lionel was just, like, a recruiter," Kate said.

"He was so sweet," Darleen said.

"And he never came on to us," Kate said. "He was a real gentleman."

They all nodded agreement.

"And cute," Kelly said.

"That's important," Amy said. "Wouldn't want to waste it on an ugly guy."

They laughed happily.

"You all know Lionel?" I said.

They did.

"It's getting on toward business hours, ladies," April said. "Is there anything else?"

"What's going to happen?" Darleen said.

I smiled at her.

"In general?" I said. "Or as regards Ollie DeMars?"

"Are we going to be safe here?"

"Probably."

"Will it come out about us?" Darleen said.

"No one wants to out you unless we have to," I said.

"Why would you have to?" Darleen said.

All the women, including April, I thought, had tensed up again.

"No reason I can think of," I said. "As long as everyone tells me the truth."

Darleen looked at me carefully.

"But if we told you the truth and had to be a witness, or something," she said, "wouldn't that be worse?"

"I was hoping you wouldn't think of that," I said.

"So we are not your first priority," Darleen said.

"Darleen," April said.

"No," Darleen said. "I want an answer."

The others agreed with Darleen. I took in a little air.

"My primary purpose here is to help April. But Ollie DeMars is part of whatever threat there is, and I need to figure out who killed him so that I can figure out how best to help April. Collateral beneficiaries of anything good I can do for April would appear to be you. All of you."

"Would you sacrifice one of us to help April?"

"Probably," I said. "But we're now getting into one of those hypothetical realms, like if you had two children and both were drowning and you could only save one, which one would you save."

Darleen nodded.

"But," she said, "we actually might drown, we need to know."

"You can't," I said. "It's a question without context. I don't know enough. I can only do what I can do. And I can only do that when it's time to do it."

The room was silent. I didn't blame it. I sounded metaphysical, even to myself.

Then Amy said, "At least he's not lying to us."

Darleen shook her head.

"They all lie to us," she said.

·34·

Ollie's clubhouse was locked. There was a big crime-scene sign on the door. But I had a key from Belson, and unlocked the door, and strolled brazenly in. I closed the door behind me and turned the bolt. It was very quiet. The only sound was the hum of the refrigerator against the wall of the outer room. The crime-scene people had dusted for prints and collected and bagged and photographed and studied and gone through the place like they were auditioning for *CSI: South Boston*. I didn't have to be careful. I opened the refrigerator door. It was empty. I looked around the room. It looked the same as it had. There were two windows. Each of them had a thick security screen. I walked down the short hall. At the end was a small bathroom. I looked in. It was empty of everything except the toilet and the sink. I went into Ollie's office. Nothing different. I looked around.

There was a security screen over the window in Ollie's office. There were no other windows. No doors but the front one. I opened Ollie's desk drawer. Crime Scene had cleaned it out. The wastebasket was empty. I went back to the front door and began to walk through it.

Okay. Killer came in here. No one's here, or they are here and they leave, for whatever reason. TV might be on, might not. I walk across the room. Even if I've never been here before, there's no place else to go. Down the hall. Ollie's door is open. I go in. He is at his desk. He sees me. He doesn't open the drawer. Doesn't go for his gun. I walk over. Do I talk? Does he talk? Do I have the gun out? Do I take it out? Whatever happened, I am right across the desk, I lean forward a little, point my gun in front of me, and plug him in the forehead right above his nose. I pantomimed the shot. He snaps back, bounces forward, starts bleeding onto his shirt. I put the gun away. Turn around and walk out? Why would I stick around? Somebody might have heard the shot. Unless he had something I wanted. Crime Scene found no sign of anyone looking for anything. No way to know. Anyway, as soon as I can, I leave. I walk back down the hall, out through the lounge, and out the front door.

I stood at the front door and then turned around and looked at everything again. Nothing spoke to me. I went to one of the ratty chairs in front of the TV and sat and looked at the room and the hall. Nothing. I'd seen Belson do this for an hour. Simply sit and look until he saw something. Or until he was certain there was nothing to see. It was more than close observation. I always suspected that if he did it long enough, he'd begin to intuit what happened. He never said so. But I was always suspicious.

Ollie DeMars was a rough guy in a rough business. He would not sit here at night alone in an unlocked building and allow somebody to wander in and shoot him. He had to have known the shooter. The slug they dug out of him was a. 22. *A woman's gun? Or was I being a sexist oinker?* A woman made some sense, though. If he was expecting someone to come in and haul his ashes, maybe he'd send people away, and maybe he'd let a woman walk in and shoot him at close range. ME had said there was no indication of sexual activity. Which meant only that she'd gotten right to the shooting. If she was a she. Lionel was the kind of guy might use a. 22, nothing big and heavy that might break the line of his suit. Or it might be some pro trying to confuse us. *If so, what happened to Ollie's crew? Did they sell him out? Were they frightened away? If it was a woman, was it April? Why would she shoot him? We'd already chased him off. Could she shoot him?* It was hard to figure April. She had not lived like most people.

Maybe it had nothing to do with anything I knew anything about. Ollie was a freelancer and busy. It could have nothing to do with me. But assuming that didn't lead anywhere. I wanted it to go somewhere. Things didn't make sense enough for me to leave it be. I didn't want to blow April's cover. But I wasn't exactly clear on what she was covering. I understood why she and her professional staff wanted to stay off the screen. She was running an illegal enterprise, and if it went public, the cops would be obliged to bust her. I didn't care about the illegal enterprise. Prostitution was probably bad for a lot of prostitutes. But it seemed pretty good to the group I was dealing with. And I had a limited attention span for larger issues. Smaller ones were hard enough.

I sat for a while longer in the silent room, made more silent by the white sound of the refrigerator. I let the silence sink in, looking for an intuition. I didn't get one. Maybe Belson never did, either.

·35·

I was back in New York. I had spent so much time in New York on this thing that people were beginning to greet me on the street. Spenser, Mr. Broadway.

It was the middle of February. The sun was bright. The snow had melted except in occasional shady lees. Either spring was early this year or the gods were making sport of us. The gods seemed more likely. On the other hand, pitchers and catchers had reported in Florida. And the first spring training game was only fifteen days away.

I met Patricia Utley for lunch uptown at Café Boulud. She had a glass of white wine. I had a Virgin Mary.

"You still in the same place?" I said, just to say something.

"No, after Stephen died, I moved a little east," she said, "and a little uptown."

"He was more than a bodyguard," I said.

"Yes," Patricia Utley said. "He was."

"Do you have someone now?"

"I have a security man who works the house when there are clients. He's very capable."

"I hear a *but*," I said.

"But he is not there except during business hours. He is not Stephen."

"I'm sorry," I said.

"Love makes you vulnerable," she said.

"Better than not love," I said.

"Yes," she said. "That's probably true. I'm glad I didn't miss it."

It was the first time she had ever alluded to a relationship with Stephen. We were quiet. The room was comfortably full but not noisy, with no sense of crowd.

"Is someone paying you for all of this?" she said when her wine arrived.

"Goodness is its own reward," I said.

She took a small sip and enjoyed it. Then she smiled at me.

"No," she said. "It isn't."

"It's not?" I said. "You mean I've been living a lie?"

"Sadly, yes," Patricia Utley said. "Is there more trouble with April?"

I nodded.

"And you need something from me on that score?"

"Maybe," I said.

She nodded and sipped some wine. I drank some Virgin Mary. I didn't like it, but it was there. Susan contended that I drank automatically, and that if I were given turnip juice, I would drink five glasses.

"I have gone nearly as far as I care to with April," Patricia Utley said. "I had very little reason to go anywhere with her. But years ago, when you brought her to me, I relaxed my cynicism enough to get caught up in your Goody Two-shoes passion."

"Goody Two-shoes?"

"I have been in the flesh trade in New York City for thirty years," she said. "I have earned my cynicism. I know in your own way you are probably more cynical than I am. Yet it hasn't made you cynical."

"You might be losing me," I said.

"No," she said, "I'm not. You may be the smartest person I have ever met. You understand me fine. I am not ready to give April too much more line."

"She fell in love again," I said.

"Oh, good God," Patricia Utley said.

"Guy named Lionel Farnsworth," I said.

She nodded.

"Yes, he always requested her. Then he stopped."

"She was giving him freebies," I said.

"Always a risk," Patricia Utley said.

"When you sent her up to Boston, he came along, cut himself into the business. They've been skimming. Putting aside the down payment so they could start a chain of their own boutique cathouses. Farnsworth says he has the rest of the financing in place."

Patricia Utley nodded.

"And," she said, "has she given the skimmed savings to Lionel?"

"I don't know, but what would you guess?"

"We both know she has," Patricia Utley said.

"We do," I said.

Maybe my cynicism had made me cynical after all. Our salads arrived. We paused while they were served. Patricia Utley ordered a second glass of wine. I had another Virgin Mary.

"According to April, Lionel cheated on her. She broke it off. He wanted his share of everything. She refused. He hired some bad guys. And now the guy he hired has been murdered."

"Oh dear," Patricia Utley said. "That means police."

"Yep. I've got some pull. The cops are willing to let April stay below the radar for now."

"And you've talked with Lionel?"

"Yes."

"How does his story jibe with April's?"

"Not as well as one would wish."

Patricia Utley smiled sadly and nodded. The drinks arrived.

"What would you have me do?" Patricia Utley said when we were alone.

"What do you know about Farnsworth?" I said.

"Probably less than you. The girls liked him, April obviously. But the other girls he was with. They all said he was charming and gentlemanly."

"Did he continue to patronize your establishment after he stopped requesting April?"

"Yes."

"He have other favorites?"

She was silent for a moment, thinking about something.

"Yes," she said.

"You ever open up any other, ah, branch offices like you did with April?"

She was silent for a longer while and then began to nod slowly. I found myself nodding with her.

"Goddamn," she said.

"Not all of his favorites opened up boutiques of their own," I said.

Patricia nodded.

"But all of the people in business for themselves had been favorites of Lionel," I said.

She nodded again.

"Thirty years," she said, "making it big in a tough business, and I'm getting hustled."

"Humbling," I said. "Isn't it."

"That sonova bitch," Patricia Utley said.

"I'll need to talk with those women," I said.

Patricia Utley nodded.

"Of course," she said.

I ate my salad. Every time I turned a corner, the truth seemed to have turned the next corner, just out of sight.

"That sonova fucking bitch," she said.

I finished my salad.

"My sentiments exactly," I said.

·36·

Alana Adler's mansion was in a brick rowhouse in Philadelphia, not far from Logan Square. I always liked Philly. It felt like Boston, only bigger. I went into the rowhouse.

"My name is Spenser," I said to the receptionist. "I have an appointment with Ms. Adler."

"Have a seat, please," the receptionist said. "I'll let her know you're here."

I sat in the chair provided. The receptionist sat at her desk. Except for the announcement of my arrival, everything was very quiet. The place was so starchy, I felt like I was going to the principal's office. After a few motionless, soundless moments, a door opened and a woman came into the room.

"Mr. Spenser?" she said.

"Yes."

"Mrs. Utley told me to expect you. Come on in."

Easy so far.

The room I entered was a small sitting room. There were heavy drapes, Tiffany lamps, a two-person love seat, a couple of club chairs, and a small antique writing table that Alana apparently used as a desk. She sat at it. I chose a club chair. We were at street level, and through the window you could watch people strolling by.

"How can I help you," Alana said.

She looked like a mature cheerleader. Probably in her late forties. She had a pretty face; short, blond hair; and a sturdy and serviceable-looking body. She was wearing a black turtleneck sweater and a gray pantsuit. Her heels were very high.

"Do you know Lionel Farnsworth?" I said.

The lines around her mouth deepened as if she were setting her jaw. It didn't look very effective, given the soft cuteness of her cheerleader face.

She shrugged.

"Did Mrs. Utley tell you why I'm interested in him?" I said.

"She said he is suspected of some, um, irregularities," she said.

"Before you became an executive," I said, "when you were working out of Mrs. Utley's house, you were one of the girls he often requested."

"Yes," she said.

"You know now why that is?"

"I was good at what I did," she said.

She smiled a little and thought about it.

"Actually," she said, "I still am."

"Do you and he have any sort of relationship now?" I said.

"Like what?"

I smiled.

"Like any sort," I said.

"Well, I see him now and then when he's in Philadelphia."

"Professionally?" I said.

"No, no. We're friends."

"Friends with benefits?" I said.

"I'm not sure that's your business."

"Does seem kind of nosy, doesn't it?" I said.

"On the other hand, I am hardly a virgin," she said.

"There's that," I said. "Did you know he also has a friend in Boston? And one in New Haven?"

"What do you mean?"

"I mean Lionel snuggles up to people that he wishes to exploit."

"Exploit?"

"Has he shared his dream with you?" I said. "Dreamgirl? A chain of boutique sex mansions across America, appealing to all those upscale sophisticates who used to join Playboy clubs?"

She stared at me.

"Love like a playboy," I said.

"He told you this?"

I smiled enigmatically. At least I hoped it was enigmatic. I was never exactly sure about my enigmatic smile.

"Mrs. Utley opened up a branch in Boston, one in New Haven, one here. Probably trying to capture the Ivy League market. Each is headed by one of her former working girls. April Kyle in Boston, Kristen LeClaire in New Haven. You here. Lionel has a relationship with each of you."

Alana stared at me. The lines that had appeared around her mouth had hardened.

"I would bet that you and he are planning to cut your ties to Mrs. Utley at an appropriate time and set up your own chain. From sea to shining sea."

She shook her head. Not so much in denial, I thought, as in disbelief.

"He can do the financing," I said. "But you have to come up with a down payment, and to acquire that quickly, he has helped you skim some earnings off the top and defraud Mrs. Utley."

"He has a relationship with April?"

"Yes."

"And Kristen?" Alana said.

"Yes."

"He told each of them those same things?"

"Yes."

We were quiet. I could feel the pressure of soundlessness in the house. I thought of the receptionist sitting in the reception room in the imperative silence. It was like being entombed. Then Alana began to breathe as if it were difficult and tears began to roll down her face. She didn't cover her face or say anything. She sat breathing hard with the tears flowing silently.

"Yeah," I said. "April and Kristen had pretty much the same thing to say."

·37·

Susan and I had a Valentine's Day supper at Aujour-d'hui, the dining room at the Four Seasons Hotel. It was the right kind of place for such a supper. The ceilings were high, the lights were muted, the service was friendly and well executed, the food was good, and the window-wall view of the Public Garden was all that the architect had probably hoped it would be. Many of the dining-room staff knew Susan and stopped to talk with her. None of them knew me, but they treated me as if they did because I was with her.

I didn't mind. There were circles where people knew me better. Of course, they weren't circles anyone wanted to move in.

We began with cocktails. Cosmopolitan for Susan. Martini for me, on the rocks, with a twist. When we were alone and it was safe, we exchanged poems written expressly for the occasion, as we always did. Susan's poem, like all her poems, began "roses are red, violets are blue" and went on through odd rhymes and strange metaphors to say very touching things, some of which were quite funny and some of which were quite obscene. My poetry was, of course, Miltonesque . . . in a vulgar sort of way. She read hers aloud, though softly, and I read mine the same. When we were through we leaned across the table and kissed each other lightly, and settled back to read the menu.

"Do you ever throw your poems from me away?"

"Of course not," I said.

"I keep yours, too."

"After we're gone," I said, "what do you suppose people will think?"

"That we were foul-mouthed, oversexed, and clever," Susan said.

"Not a bad obit," I said.

The waiter came with his pad.

"How was your trip," she said to me after we had ordered.

I told her.

She frowned and took a small sip of Cosmopolitan.

"Isn't this beginning to give you a headache?" she said.

"In the memorable words of L'il Abner," I said, "'Confusin', but not amusin'.'"

"It's beginning to sound like one of those tumultuous medieval paintings of hell, where it's not easy to see who is doing what to whom."

"People aren't always being open and frank with me," I said. "But the best I can figure is that Mrs. Utley wanted to branch out. Lionel cut in on it and has seduced these three experienced professionals to think he loves them so they'll help him steal Mrs. Utley's money."

"What about his dream of going national?" Susan said. "Is that real or persiflage."

"Yikes," I said. "Persiflage."

"Must I continuously remind you," Susan said, "that I went to Harvard?"

"I love you anyway," I said. "I don't know about his dream."

"What about Ollie DeMars?" Susan said. "If April was in this with Lionel Whosis, why did Lionel Whosis hire Ollie to harass her, and why did she hire you to prevent it?"

"Don't know."

"Who killed Ollie?"

"Don't know."

The waiter came by and looked at my empty glass. I nodded. He went to get me another martini.

"What do you know for sure?" she said.

"That everybody I have talked to so far has lied to me."

"Even Mrs. Utley?"

I shrugged.

"Maybe," I said. "I can't be sure she hasn't."

"It does seem clear that Lionel is trying to pull off some scheme."

"Yes."

"And all of the people he's to pull it off with," Susan said, "or on, or however one says it, are women."

I nodded.

"Wasn't he the one you found because he'd been in jail?"

"Yeah. Real-estate scam," I said.

"Do you know who he scammed?" Susan said.

"You mean specifically?"

"Yes."

I shook my head.

"Maybe you should find out," Susan said. "I wouldn't be amazed to find that they were women, too."

"You think there's some sort of misogyny at work?" I said.

"Maybe he just finds them easier targets," Susan said. "But maybe he likes to fuck them."

"You mean that literally," I said.

"I do," she said, "but also colloquially, in the sense of *fuck them up*."

"It's a pattern," I said.

"It would be interesting to find it was an even wider pattern," Susan said.

"So what would I know, if I knew that?" I said.

My martini arrived. I took a sip.

"I do the strategic thinking," Susan said. "Up to you to implement it."

"My God," I said. "You did go to Harvard."

She smiled at me and raised her glass. I touched it with mine.

"At the moment, the assumption is that Lionel is doing this for money," Susan said. "If you found reason to think he might be doing this out of misogynistic pathology, or for both reasons, you'd know something you don't know now."

I nodded. We sat for a minute, enjoying us.

"Well," I said. "Better to know than not know."

"Much," Susan said.

·38·

I was downtown on the second floor of the Moynihan Federal Courthouse, in the Open Records department with Corsetti. In front of me was an enormous case file in a big cardboard box.

"Don't look at me," Corsetti said. "I got you in here. Wading through that slop is up to you."

"You're just going to sit there?"

"Yeah."

"And do nothing?"

"I might put my feet up," Corsetti said, "and kind of squinch my eyes half shut and rest and look to see if any good-looking broads come through here."

"Nothing has happened so far," I said, "to make me think they will."

Corsetti grinned at me and tilted his chair back and put his feet up and appeared to close his eyes.

"Let's see," he said.

I began to lumber through the file. After ten minutes, I felt that I might be facing extinction. If the dinosaurs had not been exterminated by a meteor, a few hours reading the language of the law would have done it. Corsetti was motionless but alert except for some periods when he snored. By late afternoon I had extracted six names and addresses from the quicksand of documents. All of the names were female. All of them were in the tristate area.

I tapped Corsetti's foot. He opened his eyes.

"See any good-looking women?" I said.

"None," Corsetti said.

"Maybe on the ride uptown," I said.

"East Side or West Side?" Corsetti said.

"Sutton Place," I said.

"There'll be some for sure," Corsetti said.

"You ever actually do any work for the NYPD?" I said to Corsetti as he drove us up the FDR.

"Keeping an eye on you," Corsetti said, "is a real example of protection and service."

"And you might get to bust somebody down here, one of these days."

"Would that be a thrill," Corsetti said, "or what?"

"There's at least one homicide involved," I said.

"In Boston."

"But it may have connections down here," I said.

"Long as you keep buying me lunch," Corsetti said.

"In the service of justice," I said, "mind if I use your name?"

"Hell no," Corsetti said.

I took out my cell phone and dialed a number.

"Mrs. Carter?" I said. "This is detective Eugene Corsetti, New York police."

"Yes?"

"I'm still tying up some loose ends on that real-estate case you were involved in."

"I thought that was all over and the bastard went to jail."

"I'll explain when I get there," I said. "Just routine follow-up. Nothing for you to worry about. Just wanted to know that you'd be there."

"I'm here," she said. "It's nothing bad, is it?"

"No, no," I said. "My partner and I will see you soon."

"My partner," Corsetti said. "Nice. So when we go there she'll think you're a cop, too."

"You can tell her the truth," I said.

"I try not to," Corsetti said. "If I don't have to."

Corsetti pulled up and parked on 52nd Street in front of an apartment near the river. He put the cop light on top of the cruiser.

"Keep the fucking traffic buzzards from hauling it off to the tow lot," he said. "Who we going to see?"

"Woman named Norah Carter," I said. "One of the people defrauded by Farnsworth."

"I guess he didn't get it all," Corsetti said as we waited for the elevator in Norah Carter's building. "Living around here costs more than you and I could scrape up together."

The elevator door opened. We stepped in. I punched 6. The door closed.

"How do you know I'm not rich?" I said.

"I've seen how you dress," Corsetti said.

· 39 ·

Norah Carter was maybe fifty-two, a little overweight but pulled together okay, and pretty, given an age and weight discount. Corsetti showed her his badge. She let us in, and we sat in her living room.

"My," she said. "Two formidable-looking men right here in my living room."

She offered coffee. We declined. She checked Corsetti's left hand and mine. Corsetti wore a wedding ring. Her interest shifted subtly to me.

"You were one of the people that Lionel Farnsworth swindled," I said.

She blushed a little and looked down at her lap.

"Oh, that," she said. "That thing about condos."

"Can you tell us about that?" I said.

"Oh," she said. "My. Well . . ." She raised her eyes. "I guess I have no sense about men. Larry—I knew him as Larry Farley—seemed so nice."

"How'd you meet him?" I said.

She went back to looking down.

"It's embarrassing," she said. "He picked me up in a bar."

"In the neighborhood?" I said.

"Yes. A very nice bar. Very, ah, upscale. Not some kind of meat rack or anything."

"You were having a drink by yourself," I said.

"Yes, at the bar, in the late afternoon. It was always the loneliest time for me. I'd just been divorced. . . . I don't know if either of you has been through that?"

Neither Corsetti nor I said anything. Norah Carter raised her eyes.

"Well, it's crazy time. I was desperately unhappy. Lonely. Unsure of myself as a woman."

We nodded.

"The bar, Lily's, is on Second Avenue," she said. "A nice bar where a lot of single people can gather."

"He met you there?"

"Yes. He sat beside me at the bar. He was very polite. Excellent manners, and, well, he certainly is handsome."

I nodded. Corsetti's face was entirely blank, as if he were thinking about something else, something happening in another place.

"He walked me home and didn't even ask to come in."
She giggled.

"I was in a *tsimmis* about whether to invite him in,"
she said. "I needed to know I was desirable. But I didn't
want to be some sort of first-date slut."

"Of course," I said.

"He was so kind, as if he understood," Norah Carter
said. "He invited me to have dinner with him the next
night."

"And you didn't ask him in."

"Not that night. That was what was so nice. He let me
know he'd be back anyway."

"And you had dinner," I said.

"Yes. Le Perigord, and it was lovely."

I nodded.

"And then he came home with you."

She looked down again. I think she was trying to
blush, but no color was showing.

"Yes," she said.

She raised her eyes again and looked straight at me.
The wedding ring had apparently made Corsetti a non-
person. If Corsetti minded, he wasn't showing it.

"And how long after that did the subject of condos in
Jersey come up?" I said.

"We saw each other once or twice a week for several
months. It probably was at least a month before he suggested it. He said it was going to be a bonanza. He said
he liked me enough to want me to benefit from a sure
thing. It would make me financially secure for life."

"Did you get a good settlement in your divorce?" I said.

"Yes. The bastard had to give me the apartment and half of everything."

"Lionel knew that," I said.

She tipped her head.

"I guess he did," she said. "We talked about everything. Most people after they are divorced talk about the divorce for a while."

"What was the plan?" I said.

"About the condos?"

"Yes."

"He said he knew where to get some properties cheap from people who had to sell. He'd buy them for me. Condoize them for me, and I'd have income for life. He guaranteed a positive cash flow."

"So you gave him some money," I said.

"Yes."

"And?"

"After a month I got what I thought was my first rent check."

"And after another month?" I said.

"Nothing."

"When did he stop seeing you," I said.

"After the first rent check."

"Which was just a little bit of your own money."

"Yes. There were no condos. What properties there were were uninhabitable or couldn't be developed because of permit problems, or . . ."

She shrugged.

"I turned it all over to my lawyer," she said.

"Did you ever go to his place?"

"No. He said every penny he had was tied up in this real-estate project and he lived in one room. He said it would be embarrassing to him if I saw it."

"So how'd he afford dinner?" Corsetti said.

She looked a little startled, as if Corsetti had suddenly rematerialized.

She dropped her head again.

"I felt sorry for him. I didn't want to embarrass him or cost him a lot."

"You paid," Corsetti said.

Neither of us said anything. She looked up again. This time her look seemed to include Corsetti.

"I know," she said. "I sound like a fool. Desperate divorcée, fifty-two years old, easy pickings. And I guess that would be true. But dammit, Lionel did a lot for me. He filled my empty days. He made me feel like I mattered. He taught me some things about sex. . . ."

This time she actually managed a small blush.

"He taught me things about myself. He stole my money. But I'm not sure it wasn't a fair swap."

"You're an attractive woman," I said. "There are men who could have taught you those things and not stolen your money."

"Maybe," she said. "But they didn't buy me a drink at Lily's."

· 40 ·

It had snowed, just to remind us that it was still February and we weren't in Palm Beach. I sat with Susan in the car in the parking lot at a Dunkin' Donuts on Fresh Pond Circle. The heater was going. We had a bag of cinnamon donuts, two large coffees, and each other. Life could provide little more.

"As far as I can see," I said, "Farnsworth worked the upscale bars in affluent neighborhoods in Manhattan. He specialized in reasonably attractive middle-aged women who had some money from a divorce settlement and were looking for some sort of sexual validation."

"It is a period of legendary uncertainty," Susan said.

"We had our own sort of divorce back a while," I said.

"Yes."

"I was pretty crazy, I think."

"Yes," Susan said.

"You were pretty crazy," I said.

"Yes," she said. "I was."

"And we leapt tall buildings at a single bound."

"We were probably leaping the wrong ones," Susan said, "in those days."

"Maybe," I said. "But maybe those days helped us to leap the right ones now, and more gracefully."

"You metaphoric devil," Susan said.

She put her coffee in the cup holder, took out a donut, broke it in half, put one half back in the bag, and took a small bite out of the other half, leaning forward so that the cinnamon sugar wouldn't spill onto her lap.

"He was cool," I said. "He had pretty good odds. Hang around, say, Sutton Place. See a woman alone at the bar. She's wearing good clothes. She's not unattractive. In a neighborhood like that, with a woman, say, over forty, you've got a fair chance of finding what you're after. He didn't rush things. But it worked out pretty well for him. They were paying for dinner and such, while he seduced them first for sex, and then for investment money."

Susan nibbled on her donut. I'd never seen anyone else nibble a donut. Sometimes she bought a single donut hole and nibbled on it.

"And if it turned out they didn't have money, or wouldn't give him any," Susan said, "he'd had sex for his troubles and could move on."

"Leaving no address," I said. "Or name. He had a different name with each of the women."

"Good memory," Susan said. "Keeping everything straight."

"So to speak," I said.

"An unfortunate choice of words," Susan said. "Is he attractive?"

"I think you'd find him sort of an Ivy League lounge lizard," I said.

"I'm attracted to hooligans," Susan said. "But I assume many women would find him attractive."

"Apparently," I said. "Probably why he specializes."

"Maybe," Susan said.

"Is that a shrink *maybe*?" I said.

Susan took another nibble on her half-donut. I finished my second.

"Maybe, or maybe he's attractive to women because he wants to specialize."

"Most straight men have some such impulse," I said.

"Think about it for a minute," Susan said. "In both the schemes we know about—the condo fraud and the boutique whorehouse trick—he gets women who are vulnerable and he fucks them."

"I love romantic talk like this," I said.

"Is he married?" she said.

"Not that I know," I said.

"Has he ever been married?"

"Don't know."

"Be interesting to know," Susan said.

She put the last small morsel of her first half-donut into her mouth and chewed carefully.

"Some of the women seem to have enjoyed it," I said.

"That is not to their benefit," Susan said. "But regardless, their response doesn't change his intent."

I nodded. "And you think his intent was cruelty."

"Or revenge," Susan said. "Or a need he doesn't understand himself."

"Or you might be wrong," I said.

"Or I might be wrong," Susan said.

We both drank some coffee. Across the parkway, the ice on Fresh Pond was nearly gone. People and dogs plodded or dashed along the trail that circled the lake.

"But you might want to look into his history with women," Susan said.

"Gee," I said, "I was thinking about just having another donut."

"Instead of investigating Farnsworth's psychosexual past?"

"Yeah."

"Okay," Susan said. "Then I'll eat the other half of mine."

"Maybe after we finish," I said.

·41·

It was bright sunshine, not very warm, but in
the direct sun the snow was melting and water dripped
past my window in a heartening way. In Florida, spring
training was under way in full. And somewhere, almost
certainly, the sound of the turtle was heard in the land.
Belson came in with a takeout bag of coffee and donuts.
He put the bag on my desk and set out the contents. I
looked at the donuts.

"Whole-wheat?" I said.

"Nope."

"High-fiber?" I said.

"Nope."

"My God," I said. "You don't believe in fiber?"

"Fuck fiber," Belson said.

He pried the little triangle out of the plastic top of his
coffee cup. I took a plain donut.

"Is there anything you believe in?" I said.

"My wife," Belson said.

I nodded.

"Anything else?" I said.

"Maybe Jason Varitek."

He ate a third of his donut and drank some coffee.

"That's probably enough," I said. "You got anything on Ollie DeMars?"

"I was going to ask you the same thing," Belson said.

"You first," I said.

"I got nothing," Belson said.

I ate some donut. "Me too," I said.

"Nobody ever worked for him. Nobody ever knew him. There are maybe fifty thousand fingerprints in there. Probably including the guys who built the place."

"Any of them on file?" I said.

"Hundreds," Belson said.

"There a Mrs. DeMars?"

"Yep," Belson said. "Grieving widow. Ollie was a wonderful man, wonderful husband. He left a wonderful estate. Life goes on."

"If you find the gun, is the slug in good enough shape to get a match?"

"It banged around in there," Belson said. "But probably. ME says it was fired from about six inches."

"You talk with Tony Marcus."

"Course. Tony was in his office at the time of the shooting, playing cards with Ty-Bop and Junior and a guy named Leonard." Belson's face was expressionless. He drank some coffee.

"Gee," I said. "That not only alibis Tony but his shooter and two other guys."

"I noticed," Belson said. "Truth be told, Tony don't feel right for it anyway. A twenty-two isn't Ty-Bop's style, and I don't see Ollie letting Ty-Bop get that close without at least a try for the piece in his desk drawer."

"Maybe he did," I said. "And somebody put it back."

"Guy still got within six inches," Belson said. "Doesn't feel right."

"No," I said. "It doesn't."

"You got anything from the whorehouse?"

"They all have good alibis," I said, "for the time of the shooting, except those who don't, and none of them will tell me who they were with."

"What's your feeling?"

"I don't think any of the working girls had anything to do with this."

"That include your friend April?" Belson said.

I drank some coffee and looked over the remaining donuts, looking for the best one.

"No, it doesn't," I said.

"You got any reason to think she's involved."

"She's involved in something," I said.

"Want to tell me about it?"

"I don't know."

"But something," Belson said.

I shrugged.

"Something."

"I can only give you so much slack over there. You're a pain in the ass, but you're not stupid."

"Gee, Frank."

"I'll take your word that there's nothing there. But sooner or later I'm going to have to haul everyone in and get names, and addresses and statements, and the whole nine fucking yards."

"I know."

"I can hold off a little longer," he said. "But Quirk likes to clear cases."

"Martin Quirk?" I said. "I'm shocked."

"Yeah. You'd think he wouldn't care."

"You do what you gotta do, Frank," I said. "This thing involves Lionel in New York, maybe Patricia Utley. . . ."

"Who?"

"Madam in New York, sort of raised April for me . . ."

"Did a hell of a job," Belson said.

"Best she could," I said. "I don't know what else I could have done with her all those years ago."

"Youth services?" Belson said.

"You serious?" I said.

"No," Belson said.

"So Patricia Utley was what I had. I didn't like it then, and I don't like it now. But I still can't think of how to have done it better."

"Maybe didn't matter," Belson said. "Maybe she was fucked from the start and by the time you met her, it was way too late."

"Or maybe she's a hell of a person who just happens to be a sex worker."

"Maybe," Belson said. "What else is involved?"

"Maybe some houses in Philly and New Haven. Maybe April. There's some kind of scheme to defraud somebody. Maybe Mrs. Utley. Maybe all of the above, defrauding each other. Everybody is telling me stories they make up on the fly. None of it makes much sense."

"And then you go back and talk to them again and point out where they were lying and they make up another story," Belson said.

"Oh," I said, "happens to you, too?"

"Every coupla hours," he said.

"Maybe I'll stop asking," I said. "Maybe I'll just nose around until I stumble over a fact or something."

"Think you'll recognize a fact?"

"If I'm confused," I said, "I'll call you."

"Misery loves company," Belson said. "I'll hold Quirk off as long as I can."

"Fair enough," I said. "You got any pictures of Ollie?"

"Sure," Belson said. "I'll send some over."

"Thank you," I said.

"You're welcome," Belson said. "You got a plan?"

"No."

·42·

I was in Darleen's room. It was a nice room. Blue.
A big bed on a honey-pine frame and a turned colonial
headboard. A patchwork quilt. Sea chest at the foot. A
table and two chairs, a big television, a bathroom off.
Drapes that hung floor to ceiling a half-tone lighter blue
than the walls. It was like a room in some Cape Cod bed-
and-breakfast. On the top of the bureau on the wall past
the bed were some tools of Darleen's profession. I took
note in case there was anything that would interest Susan.
There wasn't. On the other hand, she might adjust.

I sat on the edge of the bed while Darleen carefully
put her face on in the bathroom mirror.

"April says we're not supposed to talk with you except
if she's there," Darleen said.

She was leaning very close to get the full light on her
reflection.

"This is a murder case, Darleen. If I can't talk to you, the cops will come in and talk to all of you, and then there's no more discreet inquiry. Then everybody's name and address is established, and everybody's alibi is checked, and there it all goes, you know?"

"I know," Darleen said.

She put some sort of headband on to keep her hair away from her face, then did something with a face cream.

"I need to talk with Bev," I said.

"She's not here anymore," Darleen said.

She wiped off the cream with a tissue. Her face was still about four inches from the mirror. She began to apply eyeliner. Her movements were sure and experienced.

"I know," I said. "You need to tell me how to find her."

Darleen studied her eyes for a moment in the mirror. Then she did another touch and sat back a little and squinted. She nodded to herself.

"She lives in Burlington," Darleen said. "She's married."

She put the eyeliner away and got some sort of foundation stuff and began to apply it.

"What's her last name?"

"April . . ."

"Godammit Darleen, April me no April," I said. "You want to tell me, or you want to tell the cops?"

She stopped. Her face in the mirror looked scared.

"Prendergast," Darleen said.

"Thank you."

She resumed work on the foundation stuff. Maybe she wasn't terrified.

"I could call her," Darleen said. "Have her meet you someplace. Her husband wouldn't know. He thinks she sells Mary Kay."

"Anywhere she'd like," I said.

Darleen straightened and examined her work so far. After a moment she gave herself a small approving nod.

"Okay, I'll call her when I get through," she said. "What else you need."

I took one of the Ollie DeMars pictures Belson had sent over and showed it to her.

"Jesus," she said. "Is he dead?"

"Yes."

Darleen stared at the picture.

"You know, I've never seen a dead person, I don't think."

"Recognize him?"

"God, I don't know. He just looks so . . . dead."

"There's a reason for that," I said. "Squint a little. Ever see him?"

She narrowed her eyes and looked some more.

"Yeah, if you squint it sort of filters out some of the deadness," she said.

"Recognize him?" I said.

"I might have seen him around here," she said.

"Customer?"

"No, I don't think so. I think he was more like somebody visiting April."

"Know his name?" I said.

"Name? No, hell no, I wouldn't know it if you said it. I'm not even positive I've seen him. Who is he?"

"How 'bout you call Bev," I said.

·43·

I met Bev in the café of the Barnes & Noble bookstore near the Burlington Mall.

"No one will see us here," she said. "None of my friends read."

She wore a pink headband. One of those quilted down-filled coats was draped over the back of the chair. It was black and had a belt. In her pink warm-up suit and Nike running shoes, she looked like half of the young suburban housewives you might see at any mall during the day. She showed no sign of the beating she had sustained.

"You working anywhere else?" I said.

"The kind of work I'm willing to do," she said, "there isn't anywhere else."

"Consider another kind of work?" I said.

"Like being a bookkeeper?" she said. "Here's my ré-sumé? I don't think so. I like hooking. I'm qualified for it."

"Follow your bliss," I said.

"Bliss?"

"It's something Joseph Campbell used to say."

"Joseph Campbell?"

I shook my head and took Ollie DeMars's picture from my inside pocket and put it on the table in front of Bev.

"Know him?" I said.

She did. I saw her stiffen and her expression flatten. She shook her head.

"You do," I said. "Don't you."

"No."

"He looks a little different in the picture," I said.

She shook her head.

"He's dead," I said.

She sat back and looked at me as if she didn't quite understand.

"Somebody shot him to death," I said.

"Shot him?" she said.

I nodded. "Dead."

"I . . ." She stopped.

"It's a murder, Bev. I can hold the cops off only so long. Talk to me. Talk to them."

She nodded.

"Tell me about the last time you saw him," I said.

We both had coffee. Bev looked at hers but didn't touch it. She took in some air and breathed it out.

"He beat me up," she said.

I nodded. "Ever see him before he beat you up?"

"Yes."

"When?"

Again, the big breath.

"I saw him coming out of April's apartment early one morning," she said.

I nodded.

"I had been on a call, for the night. But the client had to check out of his hotel at five thirty to fly somewhere, so I came back to the mansion around six and he was coming out."

"He say anything?"

"No. He just put his fingers to his lips, you know, like *shush,* and looked at me hard. . . . But that night when I was coming back from Copley Place, he grabbed me. Asked me if I'd said anything to anyone about seeing him. I said I hadn't. I'm kind of mouthy, I guess. I got a little smart with him. He smacked me and he said if I ever told anybody, he'd kill me. Then he beat me up some more, to get my attention, he said. I think he kind of liked it."

"So you quit," I said.

"Sure. I didn't know what was going on, but there was something going on with this creep and April. I wasn't interested in getting into the middle of it."

"You say anything to April?"

"No, I mean, maybe she told him to do it. I just wanted out of there."

"Don't blame you," I said. "You have any idea what he was doing with April?"

"You come out of somebody's place at six o'clock in the morning, I got a fair guess what he's doing with her."

"Besides that," I said.

"No. No idea. You think they're in cahoots."

"Cahoots," I said.

"What?"

"I haven't heard anybody say 'cahoots' in a long time."

"No? I don't know. My mother used to say it all the time."

"Good word," I said.

"Really?" Bev said. "I just thought it was a regular word."

She was happy to have used a good word. Praise for Bev was probably generally more visceral.

"So you think they are," she said, "you know, in cahoots?"

I had created a monster. I could tell she would work cahoots into her conversations for the foreseeable future. It was sad to think how many of the people she'd say it to wouldn't give a rat's ass that it was a good word.

"Yes," I said. "I think they might be in cahoots."

"What are they in cahoots about?"

"I don't know."

"You gonna find out?" Bev said.

"Yeah."

"Please," she said. "Please don't drag me into it."

"I won't if I can help it," I said. "It's all I can promise."

"Oh God," she said.

"Her too," I said.

· 44 ·

My office door opened on the last day in February and a big guy with long, dark hair came in. I recognized him. His name was Johnny and he had worked for Ollie DeMars. I opened the side drawer of my desk and sat back in my chair.

"Johnny," I said.

"You remember me."

"Who could forget you, Johnny."

"I hope that big guy does," Johnny said, "with the bleach-blond hair."

"Don't blame you," I said.

"I ain't here for trouble," he said.

"Damn," I said, "I was gearing up to say, 'Trouble is my business.'"

Johnny sat down in front of my desk. "You're working on Ollie's murder," he said.

"What makes you think so?"

"My niece's husband is a cop," Johnny said.

"Must be very proud of him," I said.

Johnny shrugged. "Everybody does what he does," he said. "I liked Ollie."

"Somebody had to," I said.

"I hate to see him get aced like that."

"Yeah."

"He was a tough enough guy," Johnny said. "But he wasn't too bright."

"I know."

"But he was always square with me," Johnny said.

I waited.

"Ollie was a cockhound, though, that's for fucking sure. I mean, he was married, yeah. But he used to say his wife was married, he wasn't."

Johnny laughed. I felt like I was at a very small memorial service.

"I think it got him killed," Johnny said.

"How so," I said.

"Huh?"

"How'd it get him killed?" I said.

"I think he was meeting some broad the night he got it," Johnny said.

"Who?"

"I don't know."

"Why you think he was meeting a woman?" I said.

"He tole me he didn't want nobody around that evening," Johnny said. "Tole me to clear everybody out before seven, and he give me the wink, you know, like, *hey, hey, pussy's on the way.*"

"*That* wink," I said.

"Yeah."

"Was it unusual for Ollie to clear the building?" I said.

"Yeah, sure. I mean, Ollie done some rough work in his life, you know. The crew does a lot of rough work. Ollie likes to have people around."

"You didn't hang around anyplace to see what was happening?"

"Christ, no," Johnny said. "Ollie says clear the area, you clear it, you know?"

"That's not going to be an issue anymore."

"Yeah, right," Johnny said. "I forgot."

"Ollie up to anything with the whorehouse business?" I said.

"Nothing you don't know about," Johnny said. "Or if he was, I fucking don't know it, either."

"Who's going to run the crew now?" I said.

"Not me," Johnny said. "I'm outta here. I can't stand the fucking weather anymore. You know it's supposed to snow tomorrow? Fucking March first, and there's supposed to be a fucking nor'easter."

"Florida?" I said, just to be saying something.

"Shreveport, Louisiana," Johnny said. "I got a cousin down there, says there's plenty of action . . . and it's warm."

"Going for good?" I said.

I didn't think he was holding anything back. But if you keep them talking, sometimes they reveal something they didn't realize they knew.

"Outta here," Johnny said.

"So who will run the crew, you think?"

"I think there ain't no crew no more. It was Ollie's crew. He's gone. It's gone. I just wanted to clean up here before I took off."

"Ollie have any steady girlfriends?" I said.

"Never happen," Johnny said. "He had a different one every day. Sometimes two."

"Hookers?" I said.

"Got me. I just know that couch in his office was a busy place."

"He didn't clear you out whenever he got laid?" I said.

"Shit no, we'd have never been there."

"So why this night, do you suppose?"

"Don't know. It's why I'm talking to you. I was with Ollie awhile. I want to do right by him."

"This woman was different," I said.

"I guess."

We sat silently.

"You find any videotapes in Ollie's office?"

"No."

"Nothing? Porn tapes, people fucking, like taken from a secret camera?"

"No."

Then Johnny said, "You got a gun in that desk drawer that's open."

"I do."

"I'm gonna take something outta my coat pocket," Johnny said. "It ain't a gun. I don't want you shooting me."

I picked up the .357 from the drawer.

"Take it out slowly," I said.

"You don't trust me?"

"Trust but verify," I said.

Johnny stood. He was wearing a brown tweed overcoat with big patch pockets. He took a videotape out of the right-hand pocket and put it on my desk.

"Ollie had a bunch of these," he said. "We used to watch 'em in the office. I scooped this one, show to my girlfriend."

"You know where he got them?"

"No. But they're, like, real people doing it, you know. They don't look like regular porn stuff."

"Maybe they're a clue," I said.

"I figured they might be," Johnny said. "I hope you catch the sonova bitch."

"How many did he have?"

"'Bout half a dozen, I'd say."

"You know where he kept them?" I said.

"I thought he kept them locked up in his desk in the office. He let me borrow this one, but he told me I better fucking bring it back."

"I'll take a look," I said.

"You got a broad, watch it with her. Some of it's pretty hot."

"Good tip," I said.

Johnny nodded and turned and left.

$\cdot45\cdot$

I called Frank Belson.

"Anybody find any videotapes in Ollie DeMars's place?"

"No."

"His home?"

"No."

"Crime-scene people go over that couch in Ollie DeMars's office?" I said.

"Sure."

"They find anything?"

"Besides Ollie's, they found forty-seven separate DNA samples. All female."

"Anyone we know?" I said.

"Nope."

"Well," I said. "At least Ollie kept busy."

"Yeah," Belson said. "Nice to know he didn't live a meaningless life. What's with the videotapes?"

"Guy told me there were some, now there aren't. I figured it was worth asking."

"Videotapes of what," Belson said.

"Don't know."

"Who told you this."

"Guy named Johnny," I said.

"Johnny what?"

"Don't know."

Belson was silent for a moment.

"You're bullshitting me," he said. "I know it. You know it. And you know I know it."

"You think?" I said.

"I know," Belson said.

"Frank," I said. "Are you losing that buoyant optimism we've all learned to expect?"

"Fuck you," Belson said. "You're being cute again. You got something."

"I didn't have to call you," I said.

"You needed to know what we found."

"Would you tell me?" I said.

"Maybe, maybe not."

"Uh-huh."

"I owe you," Belson said. "We both know that."

"You know that," I said. "I don't."

"But owing you and giving you a free ride ain't the same thing," he said. "I have to, I'll put you in jail."

"I ever cheat you, Frank?"

"Not maybe exactly," Belson said. "But you are convinced of how smart you are, and you got all these odd fucking things you'll do and not do. I am not in deep fucking despair over the sudden demise of Ollie DeMars. World's probably a better place. But it's still against the law to shoot him."

"I ever find who shot him, I'll explain that to him."

"I find him first," Belson said, "and I find out you were covering up something that mattered, you go, too."

"I'll race you," I said.

· 46 ·

"Guy that gave me this tape said if I had a broad, I should watch it with her," I said.

"And I'm the broad you chose?" Susan said. "How flattering."

"I was told the tape was hot," I said.

"Well, then of course you chose me. What is it?"

We were in my living room. Susan had a martini. I had scotch and soda. Pearl had her accustomed two-thirds of the couch, leaving Susan squeezed up against me on the other third. I didn't mind. The videotape was in the player. We were ready.

"I don't exactly know. I haven't seen it yet. But it might be evidence in the Ollie DeMars case."

"Which involves April," Susan said.

"That's the case," I said.

"Do you have any idea, yet, what's going on with her?"

"Other than that she is lying to me?" I said. "No."

"But you think this tape might be a clue?"

"This is one of six that are missing from Ollie DeMars's office after his death."

"Do you have the other five?"

"No."

"So maybe somebody took them?"

"Maybe."

"Well, maybe it is a clue," Susan said.

I picked up the remote. "And maybe it isn't," I said. "We'll have to watch to find out."

"And it is, after all, hot," Susan said.

I clicked the remote. The tape started. There was no sound, no titles. The picture was in black-and-white and there was no camera movement. A man was having sex with a woman. It took me a minute.

"That's Amy," I said.

"Amy?"

"One of April's girls," I said. "She's a grad student."

Amy was agile and vigorous. The man was maybe fifty, pretty good shape.

"He's quite well endowed," Susan said at one point.

"It's just the camera angle," I said.

Susan smiled. "That aside," she said, "the camera work is not inventive."

I got it.

"It's fixed," I said. "Security camera. Ollie got hold of the security tapes from April's house."

"Security tapes, even in the bedrooms?"

"Apparently."

"I'll bet the clients didn't know that," Susan said.

"I would guess not."

Several times during the action, Amy's partner was full face into the camera.

"I don't think that's an accident," I said.

"I'd say none of it is an accident," Susan said.

"No, I mean the full face to the camera. I think she maneuvered him into position."

"Blackmail?" Susan said.

"I don't think so," I said. "They start blackmailing clients, pretty soon they won't have any clients."

"What then?"

"Protection. If they have trouble with a client. They have leverage."

Susan nodded. Pearl in her languor had allowed her head to slip off the couch and it now hung almost to the floor. Her feet stuck up in the air as a sort of counterbalance, and her interest in the sex tape seemed minimal. We watched the rest of the tape. It featured Amy and several different men, each of whom was full face to the camera at least once during the proceedings. Finally, it simply ran out.

"You get any tips?" I said to Susan.

"Ick," she said.

"Is that a Jewish word for wow, what a hot tape?" I said.

"No."

"It is a sort of ungainly business, if you sit and watch it."

"It's a participant sport," Susan said. "This, at least, was not tiresomely gynecological."

"Nor particularly contemptuous of the participants," I said. "Most porn is humiliating."

"You don't enjoy it," Susan said.

"No, not much. If someone says, 'I have a nude picture of an attractive woman, wanna see?' I'll say sure. If he says, 'I've got a tape of sex-crazed bitches hungry for hot sex,' naw!"

"I like a man with standards," Susan said. "What do you make of the tape."

"I can see why they would have the security cameras. Even in a high-class house, you get some weird guys. And Ollie must have copped some of the tapes somehow, and probably was going to blackmail April, or the clients, or both."

"He'd have to know who the clients were," Susan said. "I assume he wouldn't recognize them on sight."

"Good point," I said. "Just the tapes, and their potential for damage, might have given him some bargaining edge with April for something."

Susan nodded. Pearl snored faintly.

"Goddamn," I said.

"Goddamn?"

"If there was trouble," I said, "and it showed up on the security monitor, who intervenes."

"Bouncer?"

"In more conventional blue-collar whoring, the pimp sort of serves that function," I said. "Or allows the girls to think he does."

"And here?"

"There is no bouncer."

"Shouldn't there be one?" Susan said.

"Normally, you don't want to have to call the cops in that kind of operation. Unless there's a special arrangement," I said, "a bouncer is cheaper and quicker, raises fewer questions."

"So there should be one."

"Yes, there should be one."

"Does April have a gun?" Susan said.

"She says so, but you don't want to be shooting people, even if you have the, ah, ovaries for it. A murder investigation is ruinous to whorehouses."

"Did she think you would be there to help?" Susan said.

"She was in business up here awhile," I said, "before she came to see me."

"So why is there a security system and no one to enforce it?" Susan said.

"I suppose, with these women, who have a sort of mainstream life when they're not working, that it might help keep them in line."

"Are you going to talk with April about this?" Susan said.

"Not yet," I said. "She's lied to me so much so far that I want to get as much data as I can before we talk."

Susan nodded.

"Why did Ollie take the tapes?" she said. "Did he have access to the names."

I shrugged.

"Do you think Ollie was killed to get these tapes back?"

"It's a question to explore," I said.

"I suppose it is far better than having no questions to explore," Susan said.

· 47 ·

I got to Amy through Darleen, the same way I got to Bev. We met in an ice-cream parlor and coffee shop in Newton. We sat in a booth in the back, away from the big window that looked out on Washington Street. I had coffee; Amy had a hot fudge sundae.

"People hate me," she said. "I can eat anything and my weight doesn't change."

"I'm the same way," I said. "I guess we're in it together."

Amy didn't look like Bev, but she had the same suburban-mom quality. She was wearing a thick sweater over jeans. Her hair was short. She wore sunglasses like a headband.

"So how come you're just having coffee?" she said.

"Bad for the tough-guy image," I said, "eating ice-cream sundaes in public."

"If you're after image," she said, "you should be drinking the coffee black."

"I'm not that tough," I said.

She giggled.

"You're a cutie," she said.

"But intrepid," I said.

"An intrepid cutie," she said and giggled again.

There was nothing arch in her flirting. She seemed what she was. A woman who liked men. Who appeared to like me. Who liked to flirt, and who probably liked sex. No hint of depravity. Neat. Clean. Pulled together. Sense of humor. It was hard to be disapproving. I decided not to bother.

"You know about the security cameras at the mansion," I said.

"Sure."

"Ever see any of the tapes?" I said.

"Nope."

She ate some of her ice cream. I noticed that she ate around the maraschino cherry on top. Like I would have. Saving it for last.

"I get to see the live action," she said, "up close and personal. Don't need instant replay."

"I've seen one of the tapes," I said. "You're on it."

"How do I look," she said. "How's my ass look? My ass okay?"

"Top drawer," I said. "It looked like you maneuvered your companion around so he'd look full face into the camera."

"And smooth, don't you think? He just thought it was ecstasy."

"April ask you to do that?"

"Sure. All the girls. She wanted to be able to identify every client's face."

"Why?"

Amy looked a little startled.

"I don't know. She said something about a record in case there was trouble."

"You didn't mind the cameras," I said.

"Mind? No. You're stark naked, alone with a strange guy in a room with the door locked. I liked it that some-one was keeping an eye."

"Ever any trouble?"

"You mean like a client getting out of hand?"

"Yes."

"Not often," she said. "The clients are screened pretty good."

"But now and then?"

"Now and then you get a creep," she said. "One of the house rules is that none of the girls has to do some-thing they don't want to. I mean, you know, creepy stuff. Bodily functions, ick!"

"And?"

"Now and then you get some guy, drunk or stoned, and he wants something and you say no and he goes off on you."

"And the security cameras alert someone and they come to your rescue."

"Yes."

"Who would that be?" I said.

"Used to be Vernon," Amy said.

"Bouncer?" I said.

"Security director," Amy said and smiled. "Bouncer."

"What happened to Vernon?"

"He left a little before the trouble started, unfortunately."

"You think there's a connection?" I said.

"Between Vernon leaving and the trouble starting?"

I nodded.

"I don't know. You think he got scared off or something?" Amy said.

I shrugged.

"Vernon was pretty big and tough," she said. "I think he used to be a cop, maybe."

"Know his last name?"

"Brown."

"What did he look like?" I said.

"Big, bigger than you. Bald."

"Totally bald?" I said.

"No, you know, male-pattern baldness."

"White?"

"Yes."

"You know where he was a cop?"

She shook her head. She had eaten most of her sundae and was now looking at a small island of ice cream with a cherry. She popped the cherry into her mouth and smiled at me.

"Best for last," she said.

"What did April say about his departure?" I said. "Did she talk of a replacement?"

"She said she had somebody on standby."

"Was that encouraging to you?"

"Standby where? I never saw anybody. Vernon used to sit in the front parlor. He could be there in thirty seconds."

"You like Vernon?"

"Yeah. He was fun," Amy said. "He never hit on anybody. He was sort of uncle-y, you know."

"And you don't know who the standby was?"

"No. All I know is he didn't show up when those goons came in and started pushing everybody around."

"April have any explanation?" I said.

"I didn't ask," Amy said.

"Why not."

She scraped the last of her sundae from the sides of the big tulip glass and ate it. Then she put the spoon in the empty dish, patted her mouth with her napkin, careful of the lipstick, and sat back.

"I got a husband," she said. "I got a kid. I got my master's to finish up. I care about those things and I can control those things, at least sort of. I think about them. I don't think about other stuff."

"What do you think is going on at the mansion?" I said.

"Just my part of it," Amy said.

"Which is?"

"Lot of high-function poontang," she said. "When it's over, I leave and do my homework."

"How are your grades."

She smiled at me again.

"Honor roll," she said. "Both."

"I expected no less," I said.

·48·

My years of investigative experience paid off. I looked in the phone book under both Brown and Browne. There was one Vernon. He had an address on Elm Street in Somerville. I went there and rang the bell. It was a two-family house. When Vernon didn't answer, I rang the other bell. A woman came to the door wearing a loose flowered dress.

"Do you know where I could find Vernon Brown?" I said.

"Who are you?" she said. Her hair was in a tight gray perm. Her feet were in camp moccasins. Her eyes were pale blue and her gaze was sharp.

"Old army buddy," I said. "I haven't seen him forever, and I'm only in town a few hours."

"I didn't even know Vern was in the army," the woman said.

"Thousand years ago," I said. "Know where I can find him. I can't wait to see the look on his face when he sees me."

"He tends bar," she said. "On Highland Ave. Packy's Pub."

"Thank you very much," I said.

Packy's was at the top of the hill on Highland: plate-glass window in the front; small, narrow room; bar along one wall, booths along the other. There wasn't much light. There were half a dozen guys getting a jump on the day at the bar. None of them looked like the day held a lot of promise. The guy behind the bar was a big guy, some fat, a lot of muscle, with male-pattern baldness. He came down the bar and put a small paper napkin on the bar in front of me. *Style*.

"What can I get you?" he said.

"Coffee," I said.

He shrugged as if I were a sissy.

"Sure thing," he said.

When he brought it I said, "You Vernon Brown?"

His eyes flattened, as if some sort of nictitating membrane had dulled them.

"Yeah."

"I need to ask you a couple of questions."

"Got some ID?"

"I'm not a cop," I said.

I took out one of my cards and handed it to him. He looked at it, holding at arm's length in the so-so light of the bar.

"Oh shit," he said.

"A common response," I said. "You were the bouncer in a place on Comm. Ave? Back Bay?"

"Why you want to know," Vernon said.

"There's no trouble for you in this, Vernon," I said. "I'm just looking for information."

"Uh-huh."

"You know Ollie DeMars is dead?"

The nictitating membrane lifted a little.

"Dead?" Vernon said.

"Yep."

"Natural causes?"

"Nope."

"Wasn't me," Vernon said.

"Nobody thinks it was," I said. "Why'd you quit working for April Kyle?"

Vernon puffed his lips out for a moment.

"Ollie chased me off," he said.

"Himself?"

"Him and two other guys. Stopped me coming out after work one night. Told me they wanted me out of there."

"Say why?"

"No."

"So you quit," I said.

Vernon shrugged. "I'm tough enough," he said. "But I don't do gun work, and standing up to Ollie was going to be gun work."

"We all pick our spots," I said.

Vernon nodded. "Ollie wasn't mine," he said. "Not for the weekly salary they were paying me at the whorehouse."

"What did April say?"

"She was mad, but what could she do. She never paid me my last week."

"When did it happen?" I said.

"Few months ago, right after the big storm in January."

Which made it a few days before Ollie's boys rousted the mansion for the first time.

"You know who popped Ollie?" Vernon said.

"Not yet."

"You catch him, don't be too hard on him."

"Or her," I said.

"You think it was a broad?"

I shrugged. "Tell me about April Kyle."

"She was tough," Vernon said. "I had to call her Miss Kyle. Even so, there were times she seemed to be really friendly, sometimes, you know, like flirting with me. Other times you'd think I was a child molester for crissake."

"Because?"

"She got pissed if I kidded around with the whores."

"You ever?"

He shook his head.

"No. I'm a fucking lowlife, but I'm a professional, too. I never touched one. But I liked them. They were pretty good kids. Fun. I liked looking out for them."

"Tell April why you were quitting?"

"No. I guess I was a little embarrassed to cut and run like that."

"Live to fight another day," I said.

"Something like that," he said. "I didn't feel like explaining it to her."

"Know anything about the security cameras?"

"I know they had them."

"You ever monitor them?" I said.

"Nope. Only April," he said. "There was a problem, she'd let me know."

"So you never saw any of the tapes?"

He shook his head.

"You know what happened to the tapes?" I said.

"No."

"Ever have any trouble with a customer?" I said.

"Not often, and nothing I couldn't handle," he said. "You look like a guy would know. You get some guy from the suburbs. Maybe works out. Maybe used to play football or something. But he ain't used to it. And he ain't done much of it lately. And he's kind of scared because he's doing something he shouldn't, and"—he shrugged—"I used to be a cop in Everett. I been a bouncer off and on, lot of places."

"There's a lot to knowing how," I said.

Vernon poured me some more coffee.

"You know how," Vernon said. "Don't you."

"Thanks for noticing," I said.

· 49 ·

I took one last run at April. We sat in her parlor. She seemed stiff and formal. Like we hadn't known each other since she was a kid.

"I talked with Vernon Brown," I said.

"Vernon?"

"How come you didn't tell me about him," I said.

"What's to tell," she said.

"Might be a connection between him leaving and Ollie rousting your place a few days later."

"I never thought of that," she said.

I waited. She didn't say anything else.

"Why didn't you replace Vernon?" I said.

"Well, I was looking around for someone, and then, after I came to see you, I kind of thought I wouldn't need to."

"Do you keep the security tapes someplace?"

"Why do you ask?"

"Ollie had some."

"How on earth could you know that?"

"Guy gave them to me," I said. "Did you give them to Ollie?"

"Of course not."

"Did he use them to blackmail clients?"

"Of course not. I told you I didn't give him any."

"You got them stored someplace?" I said.

"None of your business."

"Could I see them?" I said.

"No."

"Did Ollie use them to leverage you?"

"Excuse me?"

"Did he threaten to use them to expose your customers if you didn't cooperate with him?"

"Cooperate how?" April said.

"Cut him in on Dreamgirl?"

"That's ridiculous," April said. "I don't know what you are talking about."

"April," I said finally, "what the hell is going on?"

"I don't know what you mean."

"You've been lying to me since you walked into my office."

"I am not a liar," she said. "I am trying to create something, don't you understand that? I'm trying to create Dreamgirl."

"A chain of high-tone whorehouses," I said.

"Call it what you will," she said. "It will be a fantasy destination for men. Elegant, exclusive, perfectly private, like a fine club, in every big city, where men can live for a few days a life they've only fantasized."

"Didn't you get involved in a scheme not unlike that?" I said. "Some years back? Crown Prince Clubs?"

"I wasn't running that. Men were."

"There are some men involved in Dreamgirl, aren't there?"

"But they aren't in charge. Dreamgirl is mine."

I sat for a time and thought. April seemed serene, waiting for me to finish thinking.

"I'm one of the men," I said.

"Excuse me?" she said.

"I'm one, Lionel's one. I'll bet Ollie was one. You're paying off Tony Marcus. God knows who else is involved."

"What on earth are you saying?"

"I'm saying you can't quite pull this off without male support, and you are trying to find some that you can manipulate, that won't take it away from you, that will protect you from other men."

"That's an absurd, sexist, male-prick remark," she said.

There was no anger in her voice, just the serene certainty she had maintained throughout the discussion.

"That would be me," I said.

She stood and put out her hand.

"Thanks for coming by," she said with a pleasant smile.

"Don't get yourself into a hole I can't dig you out of," I said.

"I can take care of myself," she said.

"You haven't done so well up till now."

She smiled at me steadily and kept her hand out.

I took her hand. She had a nice, firm grip . . . on my hand, at least.

·50·

Tony did business out of the back room at Buddy's Fox. It was in the south end, and the neighborhood had upscaled all around it, but the clientele was still all black. When I went in, I was the only white guy.

Junior was occupying most of a booth in the back near the bar. He stood when I came in and told me to wait and went back to Tony's office. Then he came back and nodded me on. I went into Tony's office. Tony was behind his desk. Ty-Bop was sitting on a straight chair against the wall with his iPod in his ear, moving to music, or the throbbing of his soul. I never knew which.

"Junior gets any bigger," I said to Tony, "you'll have to buy him his own building."

Tony was monochromatic today. Brown suit, brown shirt, and shiny brown tie.

"What you need?" Tony said.

I looked at Ty-Bop jittering on the chair.

"How much coke that kid go through in a day," I said.

Tony smiled.

"'Nuff to keep him alert," Tony said. "What you need?"

"You kill Ollie DeMars?" I said.

"No."

"You know who did?" I said.

"No."

"You know anything about April Kyle that you haven't mentioned to me?"

"Why would I not tell you?" Tony said.

"I don't know. Everybody I've talked to has been lying. You told me what time it was, I'd want to double check."

Tony grinned.

"She pay her franchise fee, on time, every month," he said.

"For the privilege of running a business in your market," I said.

"Exactly."

"How do you define your market?"

"The six New England states," Tony said.

"New Haven?" I said.

"That be in some contest," Tony said. "With a brother in New York."

"How do you do the transaction?" I said.

"Leonard picks it up, cash, every month."

"Ah, yes," I said. "Leonard."

"She ask Leonard a lot of stuff like you asking me," Tony said. "Leonard's good. He don't talk much. But he tell me she asking 'bout what my territory be, how far I got control, do we know the people who control other markets."

"Do you?" I said.

"Some. Know the brother in New York," Tony said.

"You know why she wants to know this stuff?"

"No."

"You ever ask her?" I said.

"No. I assuming she wants to expand."

"You have a problem with that?" I said.

"Not as long as my franchise fee be, ah, commensurate."

"You talk good," I said. "For a criminal mastermind."

Tony's patois kept getting broader as we talked. Like Hawk, he seemed able to turn it on and off.

"Sho 'nuff," he said.

"Anything else?" I said.

"'Bout April?"

"That'd be good," I said.

Tony looked at me for a long time. His face was unlined. There was just a hint of gray in his short hair. His neck was soft-looking, but it always had been. He looked healthy and rested and happy. If you didn't see Ty-Bop jiving to his unheard melodies over by the wall, you'd think you were talking to some kind of successful professor.

"Only time I been inside in twenty-five years, you put me there."

"You didn't stay in the calaboose all that long," I said.

"No fault of yours," Tony said.

"Hell no," I said. "Up to me, I'd have put you in there for life plus a day."

Tony smiled.

"You never been a liar," he said.

I waited.

"And you done my daughter some good up in Marshport a while back."

I waited some more.

"A while ago," Tony said. "She ask Leonard would he kill somebody for her."

"She being April," I said.

"Uh-huh."

"Before Ollie got killed?" I said.

"Uh-huh."

"What did Leonard say?"

"He say he don't freelance, so she'd have to arrange it with me."

"Did she?" I said.

"No."

"You have any idea who she wanted killed?"

"Nope," Tony said. "She don't tell; Leonard don't ask. That's all there was."

"Coulda been Ollie," I said.

Tony nodded.

"Coulda," he said.

"Coulda been Daffy Duck," I said.

"Coulda."

"Ollie's the only one we know got killed," I said.

Tony nodded some more.

"So far," he said.

· 51 ·

There was no point asking April about her discussion with Leonard. On the other hand, it left with me with nowhere to go and nothing to do. All I could think of was to stake out Lionel again. At least while I was doing nothing, I'd be bored and uncomfortable, which would make me feel like I was making progress.

Real staking out takes more than one staker. So Hawk came with me to New York.

The morning after we arrived, we walked across the park and settled in across the street, where we could watch Farnsworth's apartment without being obvious. It was brisk. There was a fresh snowfall in New York and it hadn't dirtied up yet. A lot of people were in the park. Many of them women. Many of them good-looking in that edgy, New York way.

"You seem to be studying every woman goes by," I said to Hawk.

"Make sure Farnsworth don't sneak past us in drag," Hawk said.

"All you've ever seen of Farnsworth is a ten-year-old mug shot," I said.

"Why I got to pay such close attention," Hawk said.

A good-looking young woman walked past us wearing unusually tight jeans with a short fur jacket. Hawk studied her as she passed.

"Could be him," Hawk said.

"It's not him," I said.

"Pays to be vigilant," Hawk said.

We watched her as she passed us and turned into the park. As the drive south curved, she went out of sight.

"Why there got to be two of us watching for this dude Farnsworth?" Hawk said. "At the same time?"

"You know it takes more than one," I said. "Even if he never takes a cab, one of us may need to take a leak now and then."

"A leak?" Hawk said. "Us? You ever see Superman about to bound over a tall building, stop, and say, 'Oh gee, I gotta take a leak'?"

"Once we spot Farnsworth and you are sure you'll recognize him," I said, "then we can take turns."

"That be him?" Hawk said.

It was Farnsworth, who was out in front of his apartment waiting for the doorman to get him a cab.

"Got that tracker instinct," Hawk said, "inherited it from my ancestors tracking lions in Africa."

The doorman flagged a cab on Central Park West. He held the door until Farnsworth got in, closed it behind him, and the cab pulled away heading downtown.

"Cab's kind of a problem," I said. "Your ancestors ever run down the lions?"

"They could, but they usually waited for the lion to come back, see if he brought anything with him."

We waited. Farnsworth came back three hours later and went in and stayed there until Hawk and I hung it up and went home for the evening.

We had driven down in Hawk's white Jaguar, which seemed a little too noticeable for tailing someone. So the next day we got an unobtrusive rental car and double-parked, along with several others, down the street west of Farnsworth's apartment. His street was one-way east. I stayed on foot. Hawk stayed with the car. If he walked, I stayed with him. If he cabbed, Hawk followed him. We did this for three days without learning anything more than the fact that Farnsworth came and went. He shopped at Barney's. He ate lunch with a woman at Harry Cipriani's; he walked in the park; he met a woman for drinks at the Pierre; he bought groceries at D'Agostino's on Columbus Avenue.

The hotel bill was mounting, always a cause of some discomfort. But we were on an open-ended job for which no one was at the moment paying me. So that night we ate in the same coffee shop on Madison where I'd had a tongue sandwich with Corsetti.

"How long we going to do this?" Hawk said.

"Eat in Viand's coffee shop?" I said.

"Hang around outside Farnsworth's apartment learning nothing."

"Didn't you learn patience," I said, "from your African ancestors?"

"If they was good with boredom," Hawk said, "they wouldn'ta been hunting lions."

"There's that," I said.

"Can't you think of nothing else to do?"

"No."

"But you too stubborn to quit."

"There's an answer," I said. "And Farnsworth has it."

"You want me to ask him the question?" Hawk said. "I could ask him kinda firm."

"I don't even know what question to ask," I said. "There's something going on that involves April, and Farnsworth, and Patricia Utley, and the late great Ollie DeMars, and I don't know what it is."

"We could ask him that," Hawk said.

"And if he doesn't answer and you can't scare him into answering, we're nowhere, and he's been warned."

"I could hit him until he told us," Hawk said.

"Which he'd do quick. You wouldn't have to hit him much, would be my guess. But how would we know if it was true? Everybody I've talked to has lied about everything I've asked them. I don't want any stories. I want facts."

"Facts?"

"Observable phenomena," I said.

Hawk was having a hot turkey sandwich. He ate some.

"They make a nice hot turkey sandwich here," he said.

"Brisket's nice, too," I said.

"I could kill him," Hawk said.

I shook my head.

"Might not answer the questions," Hawk said. "But maybe the questions go away."

"No. I'm going to find out what's going on with April."

"Just a thought," Hawk said.

$\cdot 52 \cdot$

We had been five days in New York. I was sick of room service, sick of eating out, sick of not being home. I missed Susan. I missed Pearl. I missed looking out my office window. I missed Susan. I missed Chet Curtis. I missed Mike Barnicle. I missed Boylston Street, and the Charles River, and the Common, and the *Globe,* and the Harbor Health Club. I missed Susan. I missed spring training speculation, and commercials for Jordan's furniture, and Duck Tours, and the Ritz Bar, and Susan. But, on the other hand, New York, so far, was a perfect waste of time.

"How long will you hang in there," Susan asked me on the phone.

"Until I can think of something better."

"You could come home and watch April," Susan said.

"Lionel's the mover and shaker," I said. "He's up to something, and sooner or later he has to do something I can get hold of."

"A parking ticket, perhaps?"

"Don't be a smart ass," I said.

"I can't help myself," Susan said. "Any more than you can."

"I could help myself," I said. "If I wanted."

We spent a few more minutes on the phone in adolescent sex talk. When we hung up, I went to the hotel window and looked down at Madison Avenue. Had April wanted Leonard to kill Ollie? If so, why hadn't she gone to Tony when Leonard suggested it? Or maybe she didn't need to because someone else had done it. Or maybe she had someone else in mind and it wasn't time yet. Or maybe Tony was lying, or Leonard, or April. Or all of them in concert.

I made myself a drink and stood sipping it at the window. It seemed that April and Lionel had, at least at one time, been engaged in trying to establish a chain of upscale bordellos, the first few of which at least they were hoping to steal from Patricia Utley. They seemed to have fallen out, but maybe they hadn't. April seemed to not only want Dreamgirl to happen, she needed it. She seemed positively obsessed with it. I was pretty sure she couldn't go it alone. She didn't seem to like men much, but she did seem to need at least one to depend on. Maybe at first it was Lionel. Then maybe Ollie. Then maybe me. Which would explain her making a pass at me. If she needed a man, sex was what she used. It was why she didn't warm to Tedy Sapp. On him, sex was useless.

I drank a small, pleasant swallow of my drink. There was a lot of ice in the glass. The drink tasted clean.

Sex hadn't worked with me, either. Now who? Back to Lionel? Maybe that was the real thrust of her talk with Leonard. Would you kill someone for me. Maybe it was a test. If he said he'd kill someone for her, maybe he could be the man who helped her. Referring her to Tony meant he probably hadn't passed the test. Or maybe he had passed the test and was covering himself with Tony. There was a lot I didn't know. But working with what I did know, Lionel still seemed the logical choice to be re-anointed. Which was too bad. Lionel wouldn't take care of April. To him she'd be prey.

· 53 ·

It was raining in New York. I was getting wet near the park, across the street from Lionel's building. Hawk was double-parked up the street. I had on my Red Sox 2004 World Series Championship hat and my cognac-colored leather jacket. The hat kept my head dry, and the jacket kept my gun dry. The rest was wet. Water trickled down my neck no matter how carefully I adjusted my collar. The jeans and sneakers were soaked through.

At maybe 10:30 in the morning a silvery Porsche Boxster stopped in front of Lionel's building and April Kyle got out wearing boots and a bright red coat and carrying a small red umbrella. She gave the car keys to the doorman and went into the building. The doorman scooted the car around the corner and came back in a few minutes, having parked it somewhere.

I wished I had a faithful assistant to whom I could say, "The game's afoot" or "Oh ho!" I could cross the street and say it to Hawk, but I knew he'd find it annoying. So I settled for giving myself a small nod of approval. Which made more rain leak past my collar in back.

I knew Hawk saw her. He always saw everything. If she came out and got her car, or got in a cab, he'd follow. If she came out and walked, I'd follow and Hawk would idle along behind, ignoring the occasional angry taxi. Nothing happened for maybe three hours, except the rain. Then April came out of the building with Lionel. They stood in the shelter of the doorway while the door-man hailed them a cab. A rainy day in Manhattan is not good for cab hailing. Even for professionals. When the doorman finally succeeded, he went back, held a large golf umbrella for Lionel and April, and escorted them to the cab. The umbrella shielded their view, and as they walked to the cab I ran across the street and jumped into the rental car with Hawk as the doorman closed the cab door and slapped his hand on the taxi's roof.

I couldn't help myself.

"The game's afoot," I said.

Hawk shook his head.

"What the fuck is wrong with you?" he said.

·54·

We parked beside a hydrant and sat for two hours watching the front door of Patricia Utley's building through the rainwashed windshield. The water on the windshield distorted things, fusing the colors and bending the straight lines of the Upper East Side. But we could see well enough, and a car parked with its wipers going for two hours is a dead giveaway if anyone is paying attention.

It was still raining when Lionel and April came out of the apartment building. The doorman got them a cab. April tipped him. Hawk turned on the wipers, and we were behind the cab as it took them back through the park to Lionel's building. April and Lionel got out of the cab and went into the building. The cab left us and we double-parked behind a big plumbing truck that was already double-parked itself. Hawk shut off the wipers.

"This detective work is thrilling," Hawk said. "No wonder you've made it your life's work."

I leaned my head back and stretched my neck. Outside the car, the rain was coming straight down and hard.

"I think I'll maintain my post here in the car," I said. "If one of them comes out, one of us can always jump out and follow."

"One of us?" Hawk said.

"Hey," I said. "Are we buddies or what?"

"Buddies?"

"Salt and pepper," I said. "Black and white. Friends across the racial divide. Share and share alike."

"I ain't tailing nobody in the rain, honkie," Hawk said.

"Chingachgook would have done it for Leatherstocking," I said.

"Uh-huh."

"Jim would have done it for Huck."

"I ain't tailing nobody in the rain, Huck."

"Tonto would do it."

"I ain't your faithful Indian companion," Hawk said.

"Faithful Native American companion," I said, "is now the preferred way to say that."

Hawk nodded as if he'd just heard useful information.

He said, "Snow nor sleet, either, kemosabe."

We sat. It rained. The afternoon darkened. The lights of the traffic, white oncoming, red departing, blurred quite prettily through the rainwater on the windshield. The rain-filtered emerald green of the traffic light on

Central Park West was especially pleasant. The doormen at Lionel's building changed shifts. People went into the building and came out of the building. None was April, or Lionel. The question of who would tail a suspect in the rain was probably moot, and we both knew it. Small talk had long since petered out. We sat, silently staring at Lionel's entrance. We weren't uncomfortable with not speaking. Hawk's capacity for silence was limitless, and I could endure more of it than I usually got. By 7:30 we were both pretty sure April wasn't coming out tonight. Now it had become a contest to see who would endure. Hawk was motionless behind the wheel. It was ten o'clock. I was hungry and yearning for a drink. I knew it took days to starve, so I wasn't yet in fear of my life.

"I've heard in starvation that after a while you aren't hungry anymore," I said.

"Ain't never starved that long," Hawk said.

The rain stayed steady. It seemed to be in for the long haul with us.

At five past eleven, I said, "Did you know that moderate ingestion of alcoholic beverages is good for your HDL."

"HDL," Hawk said.

"It's clearly bad for our health," I said. "Sitting here like this without a drink."

Hawk nodded.

"Am feeling a little peaked," Hawk said.

I nodded. We sat.

At 11:20 Hawk said, "Think she going to spend the night?"

"Looks that way," I said. "And you are looking a little peaked."

"You not looking so good, either," Hawk said. "Kinda pale."

"By your standards," I said.

Hawk shrugged.

At 12:15 he turned on the wipers and headlights.

"You win," he said.

I pointed east, toward our hotel on the other side of Central Park. Hawk put the car in gear.

"Call it a draw," I said.

·55·

I was pretty sure she'd spent the night when April came out of the building with Lionel at 11:30 the next morning. Hawk and I were there. They took a cab downtown and got out in front of an Italian restaurant on Hudson just below Spring Street. Hawk and I lingered outside. At 1:17 they came back out of the restaurant with two guys in suits. Nobody looked happy. The two suits got into a limo. I wrote down the license number.

"You detecting?"

I nodded.

"It's all in the training," I said.

"Something to see," Hawk said. "We gonna stay with April and Lionel?"

"Unless they split," I said.

They didn't. They got a cab on Hudson Street and went back up the west side.

Behind the wheel, Hawk said, "You want me to get one of those little chauffeur hats? Be like *Driving Miss Daisy?*"

"No," I said.

Through the miracle of cell phones I called Corsetti. He wasn't there. I left a message for him to call me, and in an hour and fifteen minutes he did.

"You in the city?" he said when I answered.

"Yeah, Upper East Side, near the park."

"There'll probably be a sharp dip in the crime rate," he said.

"Can you trace a license plate for me?"

"Sure," he said. "Gimme something to do. We haven't had a homicide in fifteen, twenty minutes."

We followed Lionel and April to 81st Street. We lingered near the corner while the cab let April and Lionel out in front of a building with a large ornate canopy keeping the water off of the front entryway. A doorman came and opened the cab door. Nothing happened for a moment while one of them paid the cabbie. Then they got out and stepped under the canopy. The doorman closed the door and the cab took off. Lionel and April went into the building.

When they were out of sight we pulled the rental car up in front of the entrance. The doorman held the door as Hawk got out. I got out of my side, unassisted, with a roll of twenties, which I carried for just such emergencies.

"Can you hold the car for us?" I said and peeled off a twenty.

"Sure thing," the doorman said. "I'll park it right inside the garage there and get it for you when you come out."

"Excellent," I said.

We started for the door.

"I'm supposed to call up," the doorman said apologetically. "Who shall I say."

"Same place as the couple just went in," Hawk said. "We were supposed to meet them outside, and we were late."

"Mrs. Utley?" the doorman said.

"Utley?" I said.

"Yeah. She got the top two floors."

I looked at Hawk.

"They say anything to you about Utley?"

"Nope."

"Me either."

We both stood uncertainly.

"You're sure they said Utley?" I said.

"Positive," the doorman said.

Hawk and I looked at each other again.

"You know what?" I said to Hawk. "I think we ought to get back in the car and call Lionel on his cell."

Hawk nodded.

"Agree," he said.

The doorman looked sad.

"Keep the twenty," I said. "Thanks for helping. We'll take a spin around the block while I call, see what's up. Maybe we misunderstood something."

The doorman seemed cheerier.

"Sure thing," he said. "You need to come back, I'll take care of you."

He held Hawk's door while he got in, then hurried around trying to hold my door also, but it was too late. I was already in. So he closed it for me carefully.

"Thanks," I said.

Hawk pulled away and we went toward the park with the wipers working smoothly back and forth on the windshield.

·56·

Corsetti called back at four.

"You move in the best circles," he said. "Car's registered to Arnold Fisher."

"You know Fisher?"

"I do."

"Professionally?" I said.

"Arnie Fisher is a money guy for what's left of the DeNucci family."

"What's left?"

"Yeah, we busted them up pretty good about five years back. Put Dion DeNucci upstate for life. Family business been kind of floundering ever since. His kid's in charge now and not really up to it."

"Think I could talk with Mr. Fisher."

"If I go with you," Corsetti said.

"And have you a moment?" I said.

"Tell me why you're interested."

I told him. And described the two men.

When I finished he said, "That was Arnie, okay. I wonder if the other guy was Brooks."

"Brooks?"

"DeNucci, the son."

"Brooks DeNucci?" I said.

"Old man always wanted to live in Greenwich," Corsetti said.

"Can you arrange something?" I said.

"I'll call you back, again," Corsetti said.

I hung up the phone. April and Lionel came out of the building and got a cab. We followed them west across the park to Lionel's pad.

"Mob?" Hawk said.

"Maybe," I said, and told him what I knew.

"Something," Hawk said.

"It is."

We sat some more. It was overcast today, with now and then some weak sunshine. The sun had set by the time Corsetti called me.

"Tomorrow," Corsetti said, "eleven o'clock in the morning. I'll pick you up."

"Where we going?"

"Twenty-sixth Street," Corsetti said. "Between Seventh and Eighth."

"His place?" I said.

"Lawyer's."

"Courteous treatment," I said.

"This is better," Corsetti said. "I know these people, especially Arnie. You yank him in, he's like a fucking clam until he gets lawyered. It's not like I got anything on them."

"Good point," I said.

"Pick you up, ten thirty," Corsetti said.

Hawk looked at me.

"Enough?" he said.

"For today? Yeah. Let's go eat."

"Cocktails first," Hawk said

"We'd be fools not to," I said.

·57·

In the morning, I left Hawk with the rental car.

"If you have to choose," I said, "stay with April."

"You pay the ticket?" Hawk said. "I leave the car on a hydrant?"

"God forbid," I said, "a scofflaw."

Hawk went back across the park. I waited on Madison Avenue for Corsetti.

"Don't say it," Corsetti said to me as we went downtown, "but if everybody thinks you're a cop, too, it won't hurt anything."

We got downtown easy, despite some traffic. Corsetti used his siren as necessary.

"I thought you weren't supposed to blow that thing," I said, "except as required by your professional duties."

Corsetti glanced at me as if I had just spoken in tongues. Then he grinned and whooped the siren again. At nothing.

"Oh," I said. "I see."

Corsetti jammed his car into a loading zone in front of a nondescript restaurant on 26th Street. I followed him into a nondescript entry next to the restaurant. We took the shabby elevator to the third floor and went into an office perfectly in keeping with its surroundings.

A fiftyish woman in a shapeless black dress said, "They're in the conference room."

She stood and led us to it and opened the door and stepped aside. There were four men in the room, two of whom I'd seen recently on Spring Street. Corsetti went in and stood in front of them.

"I'm Corsetti," he said. "This is Spenser."

He looked at a shabby guy in his sixties with bushy white hair.

"You're Galvin," he said.

"Marcus Galvin," the shabby guy said, "attorney at law."

Galvin was wearing a wrinkled gray suit and vest with a red-and-black plaid shirt and a narrow black knit tie.

"You'd be the babysitter," Corsetti said to a big, slick-looking guy in an expensive suit.

The big guy looked at Corsetti with no change in expression. Corsetti laughed and shook his head.

"How are you, Brooks?" he said to the younger of the two men I'd seen on Spring Street.

"What did you have in mind, Corsetti?" the younger man said.

He was a little overweight. Not huge, but soft-looking. Expensive clothes, manicure, thousand-dollar shoes. He was probably trying for a hard look at Corsetti, but all he could muster was petulant.

"Arnie," Corsetti said to the older man.

Arnie was thin and well-tanned. He had an intelligent face and a bald head, and his clothes fit him well. He was quiet where he sat, tenting his long fingers on the table-top, tapping the fingertips gently together.

"Eugene," he said, with the stress on the first syllable.

"First of all," Corsetti said. "I got no beef with you people. I'm not looking to jam you up. I'm just looking for information on something else."

"And he thinks we're the Travelers Aid station," Brooks said and looked around the room with a big smile. The lawyer and Arnie kept their eyes on Corsetti. The bodyguard looked at nothing.

"We know you're doing business with some people named Lionel Farnsworth and April Kyle. We believe it's about the whore business. We ain't vice. We don't care about whores."

"What makes you think we know them people?" Brooks said.

Arnie glanced at him but didn't say anything.

"Your lawyer and I have already discussed this," Corsetti said. "Let's not waste time."

Brooks looked at the lawyer. The lawyer nodded.

"What do you care about?" the lawyer said.

"They're involved in another case, where somebody died," Corsetti said.

"So what?" Galvin said.

"We'd be grateful if you told us what you know about them. Might help us with the killing."

"We had nothing to do with killing nobody," Brooks said. Nobody paid him any attention. Galvin and Fisher were looking at each other. The bodyguard remained blank.

"How grateful?" Galvin said.

"You know me, Arnie," Corsetti said. "What goes around comes around. You do me a favor, I owe you a favor."

"His word's good," Arnie said to Galvin.

The lawyer nodded. He looked at me.

"How about you?" he said.

"I'm with Corsetti," I said.

"He solid?" Galvin said to Corsetti.

"Yes."

Galvin looked at Arnie. Arnie nodded. Galvin nodded back.

Arnie said, "They're looking for money."

"Hey," Brooks said. "Why you telling these fuckers anything."

Galvin reached across the table and put a hand on Brook's forearm and patted softly.

"They want to set up a chain of brothels called Dreamgirl. National deal. They claim they already got one in Boston, and Philly and New Haven."

"They being Farnsworth and Kyle," Corsetti said.

"Yeah."

"And they're looking for investors," Corsetti said.

Arnie nodded.

"How'd they get to you?"

"Mutual acquaintance," Arnie said. "Woman named Utley. Runs a big house in the city."

"She sent them to you," I said.

"Yeah. They said she was a partner in the deal. Reason we talked to them."

"And," Corsetti said, "you invest?"

"No."

"Why not."

"I checked with Utley," Arnie said. "She said she didn't know anything about Farnsworth being in the deal. She said she wasn't in it, either, as long as he was."

"You care who's in it?" I said.

"Nope, as long as they settle it. We're not putting money into no family feud."

"So you told them that," I said. "Down at Spring Street."

"Yeah," Arnie said. "We said for them to straighten out who was in and who wasn't. Get back to us."

"They okay with that?" Corsetti said.

"They weren't happy."

"Ask us if we care," Brooks said.

No one asked.

"What did you think of the business plan?" I said to Arnie.

He shrugged. "Plan was good. Like boutique whore-houses all over the country. Upscale whores, you know. Part-time. Housewives, stewardesses, college girls, teachers, that sort of thing. Plaid skirts, cashmere sweaters. No fucking in the washroom, blow jobs in the back-seat of your car. Unnerstand? Safe, pleasant environment. Johnny Mathis on the stereo. Like fucking your eighth-grade teacher, you know?"

"You talk with Utley?" I said.

"Not yet."

"What's in the deal for you?" Corsetti said.

"Fifty percent."

"Management?"

"We don't put a bunch of money in something, we don't get a say in how it goes."

"They cool with that?" I said.

"He was. I'm not so sure she was," Arnie said. "Don't know about Utley, if she's still in it."

"You think she might not be?" I said.

"No idea," Arnie said. "Long as we got our guy in place, we don't care who's in or out."

"Any other problems," Corsetti said.

Arnie shrugged.

"Stuff needed to be cleared up. Property acquisition in each city. Who had to be greased in each city. Sources of employees . . . I mean, your average young housewife in suburban Dallas or someplace may not want to be a whore."

"Hard to imagine," I said.

Arnie shrugged. "You don't invest a lot of money in something," he said, "without knowing the answers to all your questions."

"Due diligence," Corsetti said.

"Exactly."

·58·

"**How did you know** where I live?" Patricia Utley said when she let me into her apartment.

"I'm a detective," I said. "What happened to your face?"

She shook her head without answering me, and we sat in her living room. Her face was swollen and bruised.

"Somebody hit you," I said.

She shook her head again.

"Would you like coffee?" she said. "A drink?"

"Coffee," I said.

She went to the kitchen. She didn't move as if she were hurt. She was steady on her feet. I looked around the living room. Tasteful, expensive, maybe too preplanned, maybe a little too much the look of a decorator. But nice. In a small while she came back and gave me my coffee in a big white mug with a painted red apple on it. Then she sat across from me on the sofa. She looked as pulled together as she always did, which was impressive since I had arrived in midafternoon, unannounced. Her makeup was covering her bruises as artfully as it could.

"You did not come here for coffee," she said. "What do you want?"

"What's going on among you and Lionel and April?" I said.

I felt good about "among." Spenser, gumshoe and linguist.

Patricia Utley looked at me for a while. She was too smart to think she could pretend there was nothing. She knew that I must know, or I wouldn't be asking the question.

"After I talked to you last," she said, "I called her and asked her about Lionel and the other houses. She denied everything. Said Lionel had been trying to horn in, but she had refused. Said he tried to force her and she had to hire you. She said you put a stop to it. But that you seemed somewhat too interested in the business yourself and she had to fire you."

"Always wanted to be a pimp," I said.

"I know. I was skeptical of her, and when she told me that, I knew it wasn't true and I wondered if anything she told me were true. I pressed her. She became very upset. She said she was grateful to me for giving her the chance to run the Boston house. She said that she had nothing further to do with Lionel, and the harder I pressed her on that, the more upset she became. Finally I said, 'Okay, we'll agree that Lionel is history, and that he is not now, nor will he be, involved with your business—and mine.' She agreed."

The light from the declining sun was reflecting off a window in the building across the street and making a small prismatic rainbow on the wall behind Patricia Utley. She didn't appear to notice. She was looking at her hands, clasped in her lap. I waited. She didn't say anything.

"And?" I said after a while.

"She began to talk about her Dreamgirl idea. She wondered if I might wish to invest."

"Did you?"

"No. She assured me that she would not exploit our business in Boston, or anywhere else, but that she was looking for financing and, if I didn't want to be involved, did I know anyone."

"Who could lend her money so she could compete with you," I said.

Patricia Utley shrugged slightly.

"That doesn't seem a serious threat to me," she said. "This is a girl's fantasy. I'm going to be a princess as soon as I can find the right prince to help me."

"Did you send her to anyone?" I said.

"No. I have contacts in this city, financial sources. But I didn't want to compromise them. I didn't want to be the one to send her to someone who would regret doing business with her."

"She's unraveling," I said.

"Yes. Before our eyes," Patricia Utley said. "I have liked her especially, partly because you sent her to me, but . . ." She shook her head. "The life she has led is catching up to her."

"Your life hasn't unraveled you," I said.

"My life is not her life," Patricia Utley said. "I got into the sex business because, frankly, I liked sex, and it seemed easy money. And, early, I got into the management end of it."

"Where liking sex didn't matter."

"Where I could choose who to have sex with," she said, "and never mix it with business."

"For April, sex mixes with everything," I said.

"Your girlfriend could probably explain it," Patricia Utley said. "I only know that it's so."

"My girlfriend can explain everything," I said.

"You are very lucky," Patricia Utley said.

"Yes," I said. "I am."

"More coffee," she said.

"Thank you, no."

We were quiet again.

"We'll get to the bruises eventually," I said.

She was still looking at her hands. She nodded slowly. I waited.

"I got a visit," she said gently, still looking down, almost as if she were talking to herself. "From a man named Arnie Fisher."

"You know Fisher?" I said.

"I knew of him. We had never met. He told me that April and Lionel wanted investment money from the DeNucci family," she said.

"He said DeNucci?"

"No. He said his people, but I know who his people are."

I nodded.

"He said that they told him I was the third partner in the deal," Patricia Utley said. "That I had a proven track record running this sort of thing. They said that they had already established three Dreamgirl sites."

Patricia Utley shook her head sadly.

"One in Boston," she said. "One in Philly. One in New Haven."

"These are bad amateurs," I said.

"Yes. Imagine scamming the DeNucci family?"

"You spoke up?" I said.

She raised her head and smiled at me without very much oomph.

"Yes. I said I had nothing to do with Dreamgirl, that April was an amatuer, and that Farnsworth was dishonest and incompetent."

"What did Fisher say?"

"Very little. He listened. He nodded. When I was through he thanked me and said he'd like to talk with me again, if I were willing."

"Were you willing."

"I said I was always willing to talk."

I sat back a little on my chair, looking at the rainbow on the wall. It had shifted position as the sun sank and the angle of reflection changed. It had also elongated.

"And when they had lunch downtown," I said, "with Arnie and Brooks DeNucci, Arnie told them no deal unless Lionel were out. And, maybe, you were in."

She shrugged.

"And they came roaring up here to talk you into it and there was an argument and somebody hit you."

"April," Patricia Utley said. "She was crazy. She said it was her chance and she was going to make it happen. We talked and talked, but I wouldn't budge. They said it was a lock if I were in, that was Farnsworth's word, a 'lock.' And I said I was not in and would never be in, if he were involved. We argued about that some more until I said that it was futile and asked them to leave. I stood. We walked to the door. And she started quite suddenly and without a word to hit me. First a slap and then with her fists."

"What did you do?" I said.

"I was as much startled as hurt at first, and I covered up and backed away. She came after me, hitting me."

"What did Farnsworth do."

"Nothing," Patricia Utley said. "I sort of had the sense that it scared him. He doesn't seem a physical type of man."

"Then what?" I said.

"She stopped quite suddenly and turned and walked out with Farnsworth behind her."

"And that was it?"

"No, a few hours later she called to apologize. She said she had lost her mind for a moment, the way a kid does with her mother. I had been like a mother to her, she said."

"Apology accepted?"

Patricia Utley shrugged.

"I've been hit before," she said. "And, you know, I still care about April. So do you. It's why you're here."

I nodded.

"She say anything else?"

"She said if I'd think about joining Dreamgirl, she would rid us of Lionel."

"What'd you say?"

"I was trying to think still how best to save her, if it's not too late."

"I think it's too late," I said.

"But you're not sure, and neither am I. I told her if she could demonstrate to me that Lionel was really out of her business and her life, we could talk."

"Were you serious?" I said.

"I was serious about talking," Patricia Utley said. "I was not serious about the business."

"You hear from her since?"

"No."

I let out a long breath. Patricia Utley smiled at me.

"That sounds almost like a sigh," she said.

"If I weren't such a toughie," I said, "it would be."

· 59 ·

It was pretty good spring weather, so when I left Patricia Utley I walked back to the West Side. I needed the exercise. I had done nothing but sit and stare and listen and nod for days. I felt like a rusty crankshaft. There were a lot of dogs in the park, which made me feel better. When I got to Lionel's building, Hawk wasn't there. Which meant April wasn't there. I thought about bracing Lionel, but I knew I'd have trouble with the doorman, who already knew me for a phony and a Bostonian. It was late. I walked back across the park to my hotel.

In the room, my message light was flashing. I had voice mail. It was Hawk.

"Called your cell," he said. "But no answer. Figured you don't know how to retrieve messages on it. So I didn't leave one. April come out, got her car, and headed north, me behind her. At the moment I'm behind her, south of Hartford. I think we going home."

I called Hawk's cell.

"Yeah?" he said.

"Stay with her," I said. "I got a couple bases to touch here and then I'll drive your car home and bring your stuff."

"Careful of the car," Hawk said.

"I'll be in touch," I said.

After I hung up I made myself a strong scotch and soda and took a pull and looked out the window and let out a long, though tough and manly, exhale and rubbed the back of my neck. Below me the traffic, mostly cabs, raced uptown as if it was important to get there. I watched them for a while and drank my scotch. It seemed a perfect time to review what I was doing. Which didn't take long, since I didn't know. The crime under consideration was who killed Ollie DeMars. I was supposed to be interested in that. It was what I did. But my real goal seemed to be the salvation, again, of April Kyle. Which, I supposed, was also what I did. What I knew was that I wasn't getting anywhere with either.

I went back to the minibar for a refill, then I sat on the bed with my drink and called Susan.

"I'm alone in my hotel room," I said, "drinking scotch and heaving long sighs."

"Would phone sex help?" she said.

"Probably."

"Okay," she said. "Glad to accommodate—who is this, please?"

"Oh, good," I said. "Toy with me, in my despair."

"You have never despaired in your life," Susan said.

"Until now," I said.

"Tell me about it," Susan said.

I did. Susan listened quietly, offering only an occasional encouraging "uh-huh."

"So," I said, "my question to you, doctor, is, What's up with April?"

"I'll spare you the perfunctory preface about not having examined April and thus not being in a position to make a solid diagnosis."

"Thanks," I said, "for sparing me that."

"I can, however," Susan said, "make an informed guess."

"Please," I said.

"I'll probably need to use the phrase *deeply ambivalent*," Susan said. "Can you handle it."

"You're a shrink," I said. "You have to talk that way."

"Okay," Susan said. "I would guess, and what I know of her history would certainly suggest it, that she is deeply ambivalent about men."

"There it is," I said.

"Yes," Susan said, "I warned you. Everything that she has ever gotten she has gotten by seducing men, you included."

"Seduced in a broad sense," I said.

"Yes. Seduction needn't be sexual. And everything bad that has ever happened to her has been caused by men."

"In fact?" I said.

"In her fact," Susan said. "The way people experience things is not necessarily consonant with empirical fact."

"Consonant."

"Remember the Harvard Ph.D.," she said. "This Dreamgirl scheme seems a perfect expression of her situation."

"She sees it as a way out of dependence on men," I said. "But to do it she has to depend on men."

"She has moved from Lionel, to Ollie, to you, to Lionel again. My guess is that you, or maybe even Hawk, are waiting in the wings, when the buffeting of circumstance, and her own ambivalence, overwhelms her again with Lionel."

"Which it will?" I said.

"Predictions are hard," Susan said. "Explaining afterwards is what shrinks do better."

"Informed guess?"

"She'll be overwhelmed," Susan said.

"Any tips on saving her?" I said.

"Maybe she can't be saved," Susan said.

"I know," I said.

"She's had these furrows grooved into her soul by her whole existence."

"Shrinks don't say 'soul.'"

"Never tell," Susan said. "When are you coming home?"

"Tomorrow or the next day," I said. "How about that phone sex?"

"Better than nothing," Susan said.

·60·

I was in the backseat of a Cadillac with Arnie Fisher, driving slowly though Central Park. There was a glass partition between us and the driver. There were joggers. The trees were beginning to bud. Baseball opened next week. Life was quickening.

"Corsetti said you wanted to talk private, just me and you."

"What are your plans for April Kyle."

"Depends," Arnie said.

"On?"

"Well, naturally, Brooks gotta okay anything we do."

"Or his daddy," I said.

"His daddy's in jail," Arnie said.

"Yeah?"

"So Brooks is the man."

"The hell he is," I said. "Brooks couldn't run a birth-day party."

"No?" Arnie said.

"The old man's running it through you," I said.

Arnie shrugged. "If that were true, so what?"

"So what are your plans with April Kyle?"

Arnie grinned.

"You're pretty cocky for a yokel out of Beantown," he said.

"Ever since we won the series," I said. "You still inter-ested in Dreamgirl?"

"What's your interest?"

"April Kyle."

"That's it?"

"Yep."

Arnie nodded slowly.

"Corsetti says you're the real deal," Arnie said.

I waited.

Arnie nodded some more.

Then he said, "We like the concept."

"Dreamgirl," I said.

"Yeah."

"Even though the cops are starting to circle it?"

"We can await developments on that," Arnie said. "It's not a deal-breaker."

"So what's your problem."

"We're not happy with the management setup," Arnie said. "Girl don't seem too smart. Guy is a weasel."

"Ah," I said, "you know Lionel."

Arnie grinned.

"I know a lot of Lionels. Half as smart as they think they are. Word's no good. Pressure builds, they'll sell you out for a bottle of beer.

"We could work with Utley," Arnie said. "But she ain't in."

"Why not just take the idea and run with it?" I said.

"Could," Arnie said. "Thing is, we ain't really interested in being in the whore business. Dion don't actually approve of it. But this thing falls in our lap. We consider it. But we got to start from scratch. We got better things to do."

"How'd they get to you in the first place?"

Arnie smiled.

"Brooks," he said.

"Figures," I said. "How'd he know them?"

"Knew Farnsworth in Allenwood."

"Brooks has done time?" I said.

"You wanna call it that," Arnie said. "Six months watching TV."

"So Brooks likes this idea?"

"Brooks trying to be a player."

"Genes seem to thin out, don't they," I said, "as the generations proceed."

"He ain't Dion," Arnie said. "But he's Dion's kid. We look out for him."

"So it doesn't matter whether he likes this deal or not."

"No, not really," Arnie said.

"So without Patricia Utley, there's no deal."

"We might go for an arrangement," Arnie said, "where we had one of our people running it."

I nodded.

"You have people that know the whorehouse business?" I said.

"The broad and Lionel can run that part," Arnie said. "Our guy would run the books."

"Where do you stand now with them?" I said.

"They'll get back to us," Arnie said. "Why you after April Kyle?"

"I'm trying to save her," I said.

"From what?"

"I don't know," I said.

· 61 ·

When I got back to the hotel, there was a message on my voice mail.

"Corsetti. Meet me at Farnsworth's place."

Talkative.

I decided I could walk there as fast as I could cab, so I did. When I got to Central Park West I saw the police vehicles, five or six of them, including the coroner's wagon. Half a dozen uniforms were standing outside, giving the hard eye to pedestrians. The doorman was standing around in a state of proprietary uncertainty.

"Detective Corsetti told me to meet him here," I said to a thick uniform by the front door.

"Yeah? What's your name?" the uniform said.

"Spenser," I said.

"What's he want to see you about?"

"He didn't say."

The cop looked annoyed. He turned and opened the little brass door and took out the house phone. He looked at it for a moment, then turned to the doorman.

"You," he said. "Dial the apartment, ask for Corsetti, gimme the phone."

"You bet," the doorman said and did it.

"Flanagan, on the front door, Detective. Guy down here named"—he looked at me—"whaddid you say your name was?"

"Spenser."

"Spenser," the cop said into the phone. "What, okay Detective, okay."

He handed the phone back to the doorman. And jerked his head at me.

"Go ahead," he said.

It sounded as if he didn't like saying it.

When I got off the elevator, there were two more uniforms in the hallway outside Farnsworth's apartment.

"Corsetti?" I said.

"You Spenser?"

"Yeah."

One of the cops jerked his head at the apartment door, and I went in. There were technicians at work and several detectives standing around with notebooks. One was Corsetti. On the floor among them was a body, with a crime-scene guy crouched beside it.

"Farnsworth?" I said to Corsetti.

"Probably," Corsetti said. "You know him, take a look."

I stepped over and looked. It was not a fresh kill.

"Yeah," I said. "Farnsworth."

"Cleaning service comes once a week," Corsetti said. "They came in this morning and found him."

"How long?" I said.

Corsetti glanced at his notebook.

"Yesterday sometime," he said. "Small-caliber gun. Several wounds. Won't know exactly how many until they get him on the table downtown. No shell casings."

"So probably a revolver," I said.

"Or a neat shooter," Corsetti said.

"And a cool one," I said. "Fire off several rounds in a residential building and stop to police the brass?"

"If he did, he got away with it," Corsetti said.

"Good point," I said.

"You know anything about this?" Corsetti said.

"No."

"Where's your little girl friend?"

"April? I don't know."

It was technically not a lie. I didn't know exactly where she was.

Corsetti nodded.

"How about Patricia Utley?" he said.

"Wow," I said, "you remembered."

"Of course I remembered. How do you think I made detective?"

"I was wondering about that," I said.

"You got any reason to think she could have shot Lionel?"

"You know what I know," I said. "There was some conflict over this deal with the DeNuccis. But nothing should make her shoot him."

"Just run through it again for me," Corsetti said.

I did, including the part where April smacked her around.

"Maybe she lied about who hit her," Corsetti said. "Maybe it was Farnsworth slapped her around. Maybe she got even."

"Doesn't seem like Farnsworth's style," I said.

Corsetti nodded.

"Small-caliber gun," he said, "like a woman would use."

"Yeah," I said, "sure. You know and I know that most people use the gun they can get their hands on, not the gun ideally suited to them."

"Just a thought," Corsetti said. "What do you think about the DeNuccis?"

"My guess, no," I said. "Talking to Arnie Fisher, I think they will do the deal on their terms or not at all, and they don't much care which."

"Course that's what Arnie says."

"And I'm a gullible guy," I said.

"Aren't we all," Corsetti said.

"Lionel let the shooter in?" I said.

"Apparently," Corsetti said. "No sign of forced entry. No sign of socializing, either, no wineglasses, no coffee cups. Bed was made. Cleaning people say he normally left it unmade on the day they came, so they could change the linen and make it."

"So he didn't sleep in it last night," I said.

Corsetti nodded, looking down at the corpse.

"Lionel probably slept right here last night," he said. "You run into April, you'll let me know."

"You bet," I said.

· 62 ·

I got home from New York around two in the afternoon. I stood for a while and enjoyed it. The silence in my apartment. The lack of clutter. The mine-ness. I looked at Susan's picture on my mantel. She'd be with patients until five today. Then she had a seminar she was giving at Harvard. Tomorrow she was mine. I went into the bedroom and unpacked. At quarter to three, Hawk showed up and we sat at my kitchen counter and had a beer.

"Where is April?" I said.

"In the mansion," Hawk said. "I stopped by, told her I was in the neighborhood. See if she was okay."

"She okay?"

"Oh, yeah," Hawk said.

We were quiet. Hawk's face showed nothing. But there was something.

"What?" I said.

"I think she have a new man in her life," Hawk said.

"Who?"

Hawk studied the label on the beer bottle. Blue Moon Belgian White.

"How come this Belgian stuff brewed in Denver?" he said.

"Nothing is as it seems," I said. "Who's the new man?"

Hawk smiled. There was always something radiant about Hawk's smile. It came so suddenly and passed so quickly, and yet seemed so genuine in its short span.

"Me," Hawk said.

I was silent for a moment.

Then I said, "Oh, Christ."

"Yep," Hawk said. "She say since she first saw me she attracted."

"Isn't everybody," I said.

"True," he said. "She say she tried not to let herself feel that way, but she wasn't strong enough. She suggested carnal relations."

I waited.

"I tole her I tried to take Thursdays off," Hawk said. "Rest up for the weekend."

"How'd she take that?"

"Sort of rattled her," Hawk said. "But she kept her focus. She say, 'Okay, let's have dinner tomorrow.'"

"What does she want?" I said.

"You saying she might not mean it?" Hawk said.

"She may mean it, but it's been a long time since she did it for love," I said.

"Been a long time since she knew somebody like me," Hawk said. "Plus, she say she have a dream, and she tell me she want to share that dream with me, with a man like me strong enough to believe in dreams, strong enough to make them come true."

"Yeah," I said, "that would be you."

"She tell me about Dreamgirl, like I never heard of it, and about how everybody keep trying to stop her and keep betraying her but how she won't give up and all we need to be happy is to be together and support each other."

"She mention me at all?" I said.

"She did," Hawk said.

"She love you better than me?"

"She didn't actually say so, but I able to surmise it," Hawk said.

"Anything specific?"

"She ask me to kill you," Hawk said.

I drank some beer.

"So that's what she wants," I said.

"'Pears so," Hawk said. "Plus, of course, she love me."

"She say why she might want you to kill me?"

"She say you won't leave her alone. That you want to control her like her daddy did and keep her a child and won't let her achieve her dream."

"Damn," I said. "And here I thought it was just tough love."

"Parenting is hard," Hawk said.

"Did you agree?" I said.

"I tole her we could talk about it over dinner."

"So you haven't decided yet," I said.

"Actually, I have," Hawk said. "I can't kill you. Ain't nobody else can stand me."

"Good point," I said.

·63·

I sat with Hawk in his car, half a block from the mansion, looking at April's front door.

"You talk with Susan 'bout April?" Hawk said.

"No."

"You think you might want to talk with Susan 'bout April?" Hawk said.

"No."

"She knows about stuff like this," Hawk said.

"She does."

"But?"

"But since April has decided to have me killed, Susan's objectivity will be too compromised," I said. "Won't matter what she knows."

"Unlike you and me," Hawk said.

"We're used to having people decide to kill us."

"And not being able to," Hawk said.

"So far," I said.

Hawk turned his head to look at me.

"Really upbeat today," he said.

I shrugged.

"'Spose we can't just kill her first," Hawk said. "'Fore she finds somebody willing to try."

"No," I said.

"Okay," Hawk said. "So we wait. When she finds somebody willing to try, we kill him."

I nodded. We sat and looked at her front door. Spring had finally arrived in the Back Bay. The snow was mostly gone. Birds hopped in the budding trees. I was comfortable in my lightweight warm-up jacket.

Without looking at me, Hawk said, "You done what you could."

I nodded.

"Her old man kicked her out of the house twenty years ago," Hawk said.

I nodded.

"Called her a whore," I said.

"She been living up to it ever since," Hawk said. "Makes salvation hard."

"It does."

A young woman in jeans and a red fleece vest walked four small dogs on leashes along the mall in the middle of the avenue.

"The pimps got her," Hawk said. "You got her away from them."

"And sent her to a madam."

"A high-class madam that would look out for her," Hawk said.

I nodded.

"What were your choices?" Hawk said. "She wouldn't go home. She wouldn't go to the state. You gonna adopt her?"

I shook my head.

"You done what you could," Hawk said.

I didn't answer. Two well-dressed men turned into the front walk of the mansion. I looked at my watch. Eleven fifteen in the morning.

"She had it pretty good with Patricia Utley," Hawk said. "And she run off."

"She thought she was in love," I said.

Hawk nodded.

"And she ends up in like sexual slavery," Hawk said. "And you get her out of that."

"Crown Prince Clubs," I said. "Probably where she got the Dreamgirl idea."

"Being as she was having so much fun," Hawk said.

I watched the quartet of small dogs with their walker. Three of them pulled hard, stretched out at the end of the leashes. One, a wirehaired dachshund, stayed close to her walker's ankles.

"You can't save her," Hawk said. "She been in the muck too long. She fell into it too early."

"I know," I said.

"She probably kill Ollie DeMars. It's why Ollie let her in and made sure they were alone. He think he going to get his ashes hauled."

"I know."

"Pretty surely she kill Lionel in New York," Hawk said. "Ain't no one else that makes any sense for it."

"I know."

The sun was nearly overhead. The car was warm. We sat with the engine off and the windows open. Traffic was sparse at midday. The promising spring air moved through the car.

"So why don't you just give her to Belson," Hawk said. "Let him and Corsetti sort it out."

I didn't say anything.

"Okay," Hawk said. "You don't like that, I got another suggestion. Whyn't you go on in and try to save her. Give her a chance to shoot you."

"I was thinking more along those lines," I said.

·64·

April and I were in her apartment on the top floor of the mansion again. She looked as good as she had when she came to my office in the winter. Even in jeans and a white T-shirt, she was elegantly pulled together, with just enough maturity in her face to look like a grown-up.

"I don't know what we have to say to each other," she said.

"There's a lot I don't know," I said. "And there's probably some I'll never know. Everybody has been lying to me since we began. But here's how I think it went."

"What are you talking about?" April said.

"I figure it started clean enough. Mrs. Utley gave you charge of one of her spin-off houses. It was probably mostly an experiment, see how they worked. But you had already fallen in love with Lionel Farnsworth, and it went south pretty quick."

"That's ridiculous," April said.

She sat on her couch with her bare feet tucked under her, looking aloof and languid.

"I don't know when it happened," I said, "or who thought it up, but somewhere in there the Dreamgirl scheme hatched, and you and Lionel started embezzling."

"Have you been drinking?" April said.

"Not enough," I said. "Then, somewhere in here, I don't know how, you found out that Lionel was involved in the same scheme with other women—in Philly and in New Haven. And you broke it off. Lionel was vexed by that, so he called on his old jail buddy Ollie DeMars to get you to rethink everything. And you hired me to chase him off. Which I did. But that left you without a man in your life, except me. And I wasn't suitable for romance."

April didn't bother to respond to that. She just shook her head sadly.

"So you took up with Ollie. And Ollie got far enough into things here to scoop some of the security tapes. Ollie being Ollie, he probably enjoyed watching them, but, Ollie being Ollie, he also probably saw their practical, which is to say blackmail, application. My guess is he used the threat of outing your customers to weasel in on the business."

April was beginning to vacillate between contemptuous and remote. She was trying remote now, looking past me out her window.

"You knew I wouldn't kill him for you," I said. "But you also knew if I took him off your back again he'd blab and I'd learn too much about what was going on."

She studied the window.

"So you killed him," I said.

She had probably prepared herself once she saw where I was going. She turned her head slowly from the window and widened her eyes.

"Oh my God," she said.

"But that left you," I said, "right back where you were, chasing your dream with no man to help. So you reestablished with Lionel."

"This is absurd," she said. "How long is this going to go on?"

"Almost done," I said. "Lionel and you were working it pretty good. Probably because you needed her support, I would guess, perhaps for her money, you brought Mrs. Utley in somewhere along the way without exactly telling her about Lionel. He was probably going to get rid of the other girls, he said, in the other houses, and you and he would run it all, together, once it was in place. You didn't exactly tell him about Mrs. Utley. You could ease her out once you had things rolling and were in control."

April was silent, trying to look amused.

"But the DeNuccis blew all that out of the water. They did the due diligence. They found out Mrs. Utley wouldn't do business if Lionel were involved. So no funding. Even when you smacked her, Mrs. Utley wouldn't go for it. Worse, the DeNuccis wanted to control the deal, and, my guess, Lionel wanted to go along with it. Your dream would be run by a bunch of men. Smart, bad men. They got in there, you knew it was over for you. The whole dream. You went to talk Lionel out of it. You couldn't. Maybe you fought. Maybe you lost control of yourself. Maybe he threatened you. And you shot him dead."

"You are insane," April said.

She stood and walked to the window next to the antique desk and looked out.

"And then of course you had this other problem. Me. I was a mistake. I kept trying to save you, and in doing so I kept gumming up the works. Poking around, pushing at things. I wouldn't let it be. And the more I tried to save you, the more I screwed everything up."

April turned from the window and sat down at the little desk, facing me.

"So here you were, back from New York. The DeNucci deal gone. Nobody to help you. No man in your life but me, whom you desperately didn't want in your life. Maybe you could patch it up with Patricia Utley. Maybe you could find somebody else to help you. But first it was important to get me out of your life."

April rolled her eyes up and stared at the ceiling. *Resignation*.

"So you asked Hawk to kill me."

She flinched as if she were startled, and her eyes came back down from the ceiling. She stared at me. I stared back. Her eyes had changed. Whoever she was, she wasn't April anymore.

"He told you that?" she said.

There was no denial in her voice. Just the sound of surprise that Hawk had ratted her out.

"He told me you offered the usual incentive package," I said.

April nodded slowly. She opened the middle drawer of her desk and took out a. 22-caliber revolver. It looked like a Colt. She pointed it at me.

"When all else fails . . ." I said.

"You bastard," she said. "You bastard bastard. You wouldn't leave it alone."

"No," I said.

"Why wouldn't you leave it alone?"

"I wanted to save you," I said.

She laughed, though not as if there were anything funny.

"From a life of depravity?" she said.

"I haven't been a big success with that," I said.

"It was all I ever wanted. It was my freedom. My chance for a life. Money. Control. Free of men."

"Pretty to think so," I said.

"I can still make it work."

I shook my head. "Too damaged," I said.

"Damaged by men," she said. "This was my chance to be rid of you bastards."

"Except that you couldn't do it without men. Everything you ever got you got by sex with men. You can't go it alone."

"I can. I can kill you. I can go back to New York. I can make it up with Mrs. Utley. Start over. I can do this."

I shook my head.

"I don't know if you can kill me," I said. "If you do, Hawk will kill you. If you don't kill me and go back to New York, and Mrs. Utley buys your story, which she won't, you've still got your life around your neck. You'll have to find another Lionel, or Ollie. My guess would be Brooks DeNucci."

She raised the gun and pointed it at me. I waited. She pointed.

"Fuck you," she said, and put the muzzle of the gun in her mouth and pulled the trigger. Her body rocked back and then forward, the way Ollie's had. And she fell over her small desk and was still. I went to her and felt her pulse. It was faint. The bullet had not exited her skull, which meant it had churned around in there. There was no point to an ambulance. She was already dead in all the ways that matter. I stood beside her, my hand on her throat, and felt her pulse flutter and stop. I stood there for a time after it had stopped. The room was infinitely quiet. I could hear my breathing. Then I patted her throat and turned and left the room and walked downstairs and out the front door.

At Hawk's car, I gestured toward the trunk. He popped it from inside. I took off my jacket and removed my Kevlar vest, tossed it in the trunk, closed the lid, and got in the car.

"Dead?" Hawk said.

"Yes."

"You did what you could," Hawk said.

"Wasn't enough," I said.

"Sometimes it isn't," Hawk said.

Following is a special excerpt of

NOW AND THEN

***

Another exciting

SPENSER NOVEL

from

ROBERT B. PARKER

Available October 2007 in hardcover
from G. P. Putnam's Sons!

· 1 ·

He came into my office carrying a thin briefcase under his left arm. He was wearing a dark suit and a white shirt with a red and blue striped tie. His red hair was cut very short. He had a thin sharp face. He closed the door carefully behind him and turned and gave me the hard eye.

"You Spenser?" he said.

"And proud of it," I said.

He looked at me aggressively, and didn't say anything. I smiled pleasantly.

"Are you being a wise guy?" he said.

"Only for a second," I said. "What can I do for you?"

"I don't like this," he said.

"Well," I said. "It's a start."

"I don't like funny, either," he said.

"Then we should do great," I said.

"My name is Dennis Doherty," he said.

"I love alliteration," I said.

"What?"

"There I go again," I said.

"Listen, pal. You don't want my business, just say so."

"I don't want your business," I said.

"Okay," he said.

He stood and walked toward my door. He opened it and stopped and turned around.

"I came on a little strong," he said.

"I noticed that," I said.

"Lemme start over," Doherty said.

I nodded.

"Try not to frighten me," I said.

He closed the door and came back and sat in one of the chairs in front of my desk. He looked at me for a time. No aggression. Just taking notice.

"You ever box?" he asked.

I nodded.

"The nose?" I said.

"More around the eyes," Doherty said.

"Observant," I said.

"The nose has been broken," Doherty said. "I can see that. But it's not flattened."

"I retired before it got flat," I said.

Doherty nodded. He looked at the large picture of Susan on my desk.

"You married?" he said.

"Not quite," I said.

"Ever been married?"

"Not exactly," I said.

"Who's in the picture?" he said.

"Girl of my dreams," I said.

"You together?" Doherty said.

"Yes."

"But not married," he said.

"No."

"Been together long?" he said.

"Yes."

We were quiet.

"You having trouble with your wife?" I said after a time.

He glanced at the wedding ring on his left hand. Then he looked back at me and didn't answer.

"The only person you could ever talk with is your wife," I said, "and she's the issue, so you can't talk to her."

He kept looking at me and then slowly nodded.

"You know," he said.

"I do."

"You've been through it."

"I've been though something," I said.

He looked at Susan's picture.

"With her?" he said.

"Yes."

"You're still together."

"Yes."

"And you're all right?" Doherty said

"Very."

With his elbows on the arms of the chair, he clasped his hands together and rested his chin on them.

"So it's possible," he said.

"Never over till its over," I said.

"Yeah," he said.

I waited. He sat. Then he opened the thin briefcase and took out an 8×10 photograph. He put the photograph in front of me on the desk.

"Jordan Richmond," he said.

"Your wife."

"Yes," Doherty said. "She kept her name. She's a professor."

"Ah," I said, as if he had explained something.

I try to be encouraging.

"I think she thought it was low class," he said. "To have a name like Doherty."

"Too ethnic," I said.

"Too Irish," he said.

"Even worse," I said.

"I don't mean she's snobby," Doherty said. "She isn't. She just grew up different than I did. Private school, Smith College."

"Kids?" I said.

"No."

"Where do I come in?" I said.

He took in a big breath of air.

"I want you to find out what she's up to," he said.

"What do you think she's up to?" I said.

"I don't know. She's out late a lot. Sometimes when she comes home I can tell she's been drinking."

"Oh," I said. "That."

"That?"

"You think she's fooling around," I said.

"I don't think she'd do that to me," he said.

"Maybe it's not about you," I said.

"What?"

I shook my head.

"So what do you think?" I said.

"I don't know what to think, it's just not going well. She's out too much. She's sort of brusque when she's home. I don't know. I want you to find out."

There were a few questions I wanted to ask, but they were more shrink-type questions. And he wasn't hiring me for my shrink skills.

"Okay," I said.

"What do you charge?"

I told him. He nodded.

"And you'll find out?" he said.

"Yes."

"I don't want her to know," Doherty said.

"I'm pretty slick," I said. "Where do you live?"

"No need to know that," he said. "You can pick her up at school."

"And tail her home," I said.

He nodded.

"Of course," he said. "It's 636 Brant Island Road in Milton."

I looked at the picture.

"Good likeness of her?" I said.

"Yes," he said. "She's fifty-one, looks younger. Five feet, seven inches, one hundred thirty pounds. She's in good shape. Works out. Drives a silver Audi sports coupe. Mass plate number ARP7 JD5."

He reached into the slim briefcase again and brought out a printed sheet of paper. He put it on the desk beside her photograph.

"Her teaching schedule," he said. "Concord College, you know where it is?"

"I do."

"Her office is in Foss Hall," Doherty said. "English department. It's on the schedule."

"How about you," I said. "How do I reach you?"

"I'll give you my cell phone," he said.

I wrote it down.

"Where do you work?" I said.

"You don't need to know that," he said. "Cell phone will get me."

I didn't press it.

"You want regular reports?"

"No. When you know something, tell me."

"If she's doing anything out of the ordinary," I said, "it shouldn't take long to catch her."

He nodded.

"I don't think she's having an affair," he said.

"Sure," I said.

"When can you start?"

"I'm away for a couple of days," I said. "I'll start Tuesday."

He didn't move. I waited.

"She's not . . ." he said finally. "I can't see her having an affair . . . she's not that interested in sex."

"I'll let you know," I said.

He nodded and turned and headed for the door. The way his jacket fell, he might have been carrying a gun behind his right hip.

· 2 ·

It was late September on Cape Cod, and the summer people were gone. Susan and I liked to go down for a couple of nights in the off season, before things shut down for the winter. Which is how we ended up on a Sunday night, eating cold plum soup and broiled Cape scallops, and drinking a bottle of Gewürztraminer at Chillingsworth in Brewster.

"When someone says that their mate is not interested in sex," Susan said, "all they can really speak to with authority is that their mate is not interested in sex with them."

"I've never made that statement," I said.

"And with good reason," Susan said.

"It sounds like sex to me," I said.

"And it sounds like he fears that it is," Susan said.

"He fears something," I said.

"And he's reticent about himself," she said. "Didn't want to tell you where he lived. Won't tell you where he works."

"Lot of people are embarrassed about things like this," I said.

"Are you?" she said.

"No more than you are, shrink girl."

She smiled and sipped her wine.

She said, "We both uncover secrets, I guess."

"And chase after hidden truths," I said.

"And people are often better for it," she said.

"But not always."

"No," she said. "Not always."

We ate our plum soup happily and sipped our wine.

"You don't like divorce cases, do you?" she said.

"Make me feel like a Peeping Tom," I said.

Susan smiled, which is a luminous sight.

"Is that different than a private eye?" she said.

"I hope so," I said.

"You feel intrepid, chasing bad guys," Susan said.

"Yes."

"And sleazy, chasing errant mates."

"Yes."

"But you do it," she said.

"It's work."

"It's good work," Susan said. "The pain of emotional loss is intense."

"I recall," I said.

"Yes," she said. "We both do. Half my practice comes from people like that."

"Despite similarities, our practices are not identical."

"Mine requires less muscle," she said. "But the point is, you can rescue people in different ways. Leaping tall buildings at a single bound is not the only way."

"I know," I said.

"Which is why you'll work divorce cases," she said, "even though they make you feel sleazy."

"Heroism has its downside," I said.

"It has its upside, too," Susan said.

Susan's eyes had a small glitter.

"Speaking of which . . ." I said.

"Could we maybe finish dinner?" she said.

"Of course," I said. "The upside is patient."

"And frequent," Susan said.

·3·

I knew Doherty's name and address. It would not be very hard to find out more about him. He had not, however, hired me to find out anything about him. So I decided to find out about his wife.

Concord College was not in Concord. It was in Cambridge. Three recent high-rise buildings with a lot of windows, just across the Longfellow Bridge in Kendall Square. A software tycoon with a streak of vestigial hippie-ness had endowed the place with a sum larger than the GNP of several small countries. And the college, perhaps respectful of its financial base, was an exfoliating swamp of unusual ideas. It cost about forty thousand dollars a year to go there.

I went into Foss Hall, which was the middle high rise, and up to the fourth floor. Aside from my adulthood, I was too neat to be mistaken for a student. Most of them wore very sloppy clothes that had cost a lot. Chronologically, I could have passed for faculty, but once again the neatness factor gave me away. The faculty was no neater than the students, but their clothes had cost less. Hoping to pass anyway, I was carrying a green book bag. Deep cover.

According to the schedule Doherty had given me, Jordan Richmond's office was in room 425, and her office hours began in ten minutes. I strolled past the office. It had an oak door with a window. There was no one in there. I wandered past the door and stopped to study a bulletin board, beyond the next office. *Crush Imperialism . . . Film Festival: Jean Luc Goddard . . . Stop the Murders for Oil . . . Roommate Wanted, M or F . . . Wage Peace . . . No Welfare for the Wealthy . . . Keg Party at MIT . . . African American Conference . . . Concordian Lecture Series: "Apollonian Despair in the Poetry of Sarah Teasdale" . . . Equal Work Equal Wage . . . Gay & Lesbian Coalition . . . Intelligent Design Is Neither . . .* Maybe it wasn't such a hothouse of new ideas. Except for "Apollonian Despair." As I studied the notices, Jordan Richmond strolled past me down the hall toward her office.

Her picture didn't do her justice. There was a time in my life when I would have thought that admiring the butt of a fifty-one-year-old woman was exploiting the elderly. I had not entertained that conceit in some years, but if I had, Jordan Richmond would have ended it. She had brown hair with blond highlights. By the standards of her colleagues she appeared to be vastly overdressed. Glimpsed covertly as she passed, she seemed to be wearing makeup. She had on black pants and jacket with a faint chalk stripe. Under the jacket was a pink tee. By the sound they made on the hard floor, I could tell she was wearing heels.

I hung around the hallway, trying to look inconspicuous, until she finished her office hours at 4:30 and, carrying a black leather briefcase, she headed out of the building. I went with her. We stood so close in the elevator that I could smell her perfume.

On the street we turned right and she went into the Marriott Hotel. I took a baseball cap out of my book bag and put it on. Spenser, master of disguise. Then I put the book bag in a trash basket out front, waited for a moment and went in after her. She was in the lobby bar. At a table with a man. I sat with my hat on, at the far end of the bar, where it turned. It put her back to me, and I could look at her companion. He appeared to be tall. His moustache and goatee were neatly trimmed. His nose was strong. His dark eyes were deep set. His dark hair was curly and short with touches of gray. He wore an expensive dark suit with a white shirt and a blue silk tie. He was sipping a martini.

As soon as she was seated he spoke to the waitress. She took his order and brought Jordan a martini. Jordan picked it up and gestured with it at the man. He raised his glass and they touched rims. I ordered a beer. The bartender put down a dish of nuts. I ate some so as not to hurt his feelings.

Jordan and her companion gave some evidence that Doherty's fears were not groundless. They sat close together. She touched him often, putting a hand on his forearm, or on his shoulder. Once, laughing, she leaned forward so that their foreheads touched. All of his movements were languid, not as if he were tired, more as if he were happily relaxed about everything. And very pleased to be him.

They had two drinks. He paid the check. They got up and went out. I left too much money on the bar and went after them. They walked back to Concord College together. Got into a Honda Prelude in the parking lot and drove out. I was parked down Main Street a way. By the time I got to my car they were out of sight. So I went over the Longfellow Bridge, and drove down to Milton.

It took about a half hour to get to Brant Island Road. I parked on the corner with a view of the house where Dennis and Jordan lived. It was a white garrison colonial, with green shutters. The lights were on. There was a Ford Crown Vic in the driveway. At ten after eleven Jordan pulled the Prelude into the driveway next to the Crown Vic. She got out, straightened her pants a little, fluffed her hair for a moment, then took her briefcase from the car, closed the car door, and walked carefully to the house.

ROBERT B. PARKER is the author of more than fifty books, including the bestsellers *School Days*, *Sea Change*, and *Blue Screen*. He lives in Boston. Visit the author's website at www.robertbparker.net.

Penguin Group (USA) Inc.
is proud to present

GREAT READS—GUARANTEED

**We are so confident you will love
this book that we are offering a
100% money-back guarantee!**

If you are not 100% satisfied with
this publication, Penguin Group (USA) Inc.
will refund your money!
Simply return the book before
November 1, 2007 for a full refund.